LITTSIE
AND THE
UNDERGROUND
RAILROAD

Jinny Powers Berten

Illustrated by Elizabeth W. Schott

Fountain Square Publishing LLC
786 Old Ludlow Ave.
Cincinnati, Ohio 45220
513-961-6762
bertenjs@msn.com
Fountain Square Publishing LLC is a registered trademark.

Manufactured in the United States of America
Library of Congress Control Number: 2009928658
ISBN-13: 978-0-9724421-3-8

Illustrations: Elizabeth W. Schott   www.ewschott-fineart.com
Page design: ElizabethW. Schott
Cover design: Elizabeth W. Schott

Printed in the U.S.A.
First American Edition, 2009

For teacher's guide, bibliography, questions or comments, visit
www.fountainsquarepublishing.com
or email fspcincinnati@aol.com

DEDICATION

for
Theresa

A SPECIAL NOTE OF THANKS

Many people help to make a book. I had some very special readers that I would like to thank: Helen Vogt, Linda Wolfe, and Susie Heinz. My family helped too: John, Chris, Samantha, Jake, Kate, Isabelle and Poppie.

Thanks also to the volunteers and staff at the National Underground Railroad Freedom Center who gave input especially Jackie Wallace in the education department.

And special thanks to my patient, kind and humorous friend and editor, Sandy Cohan, who polished and polished until the manuscript was clean and ready.

And a thank you to Beth Schott whose imaginative illustrations catch the moment and give it life.

CONTENTS

DAN

*T*HE rain fell hard on the hills around Cincinnati that summer day of 1884. It came sloshing fitfully from gray clouds. It came with summer thunder that rolled across the sky shaking window panes and roof tops. It came and washed the statues and the buildings and the animals and the people.

Now, in the evening, it had become a fine soft rain carrying the fresh smell of farms that ringed the city, blending with the scents that came from the nearby beer factories and the canal that wound its way toward the Ohio River.

The little brown house on Liberty Street was surrounded by mist that the rain had created. The cool evening breeze blew through the curtains at the open windows and rattled the kitchen screen door. I had found a spot for myself in a rocker on the porch and was enjoying the evening peace and the lovely colors of the evening sky when my grandchildren came running to join me.

"May we have lemonade?" they asked.

"Of course," I said. "Help yourself. I just made a fresh batch."

"Will you tell us more now?" they asked, as they poured a glass and found a cookie.

"Oh, do you really want more of my stories of long ago, when I was just a girl?"

"Yes, yes," they chanted. "What happened after you found Megan? Did you ever see Euleen again and what about the farm?"

"Hold on there, hold on there. Give me a minute to think," I said.

Well, let me see. It must have been the spring of 1833 when I found my sister Megan at the Cincinnati Orphan Asylum. You remember, she had been taken there after our parents died in the cholera epidemic of 1832. I had such a time finding her. But with the help of a lot of good people I did find her and we were together again. We lived on the third floor of the school called The Cincinnati Female Academy and we both worked there after our classes. Megan was too young to do much work but she could set the tables and dry dishes. I helped Mrs. Craymore in the kitchen doing the cooking for all the students. I worked hard in school and took classes in arithmetic, geometry, French and even astronomy.

"Do you remember Dr. Drake?" I asked the children.

"Was he the one who gave you medicine when your father was sick?" asked Isabelle.

"Yes, that's right. You have a good memory, Isabelle."

When Megan and I got back to the Cincinnati Female Academy I knew that I would have to find some way to make money for the two of us. Our work at school only covered our tuition and our meals. We didn't have anything for shoes or dresses or any of the things that girls need. I had heard that Dr. Drake was working awfully hard and that he needed an assistant. When I heard that news I ran right over to his office. But as I ran I thought that maybe Dr. Drake might think it strange for a young girl to be interested in medicine and would not even think of hiring her. Well, so what, I thought, nothing ventured, nothing gained. If he thinks a girl can't do it, he must not be a very bright gentleman.

The office was crowded when I got there. I took my place in line and waited my turn, rehearsing all the time what I would say. When my name was called I had butterflies in my stomach and cold hands.

"Well, my young lady, what seems to be your problem?" asked Dr. Drake as I entered the examining room.

I swallowed hard and said very fast, "Doctor, my name is Littsie O'Donnell and last fall you helped me when my parents were dying and then I went to New Orleans where Dr. Gilbert taught me about medicines and care of the sick, and now, I have found my sister Megan and I have to take care of her and I would like to know if I can work as your assistant. I will be very dependable and work very hard."

"Well now," said Dr. Drake in his clear, powerful voice, "just hold on one minute, young lady. Just who made you think that I might need an assistant?"

"I overheard some men talking in the market. They said, Sir, that you have been working too hard, so I assumed, Sir, that you could use some help."

"They were saying that, were they? I think I can

determine if I need help. I don't run my office by listening to idle gossip. I am still able to get along without any help."

"But, Sir, not only would I be of help to you but you would teach me too. Excuse me, Sir, but how old were you when you started to study medicine?" I asked.

Dr. Drake was a little surprised by my boldness but he scratched his head and said, "Let me see, I guess I was just thirteen when Dr. Goforth took me on as an apprentice. Yes, thirteen."

"Well, Sir, I am almost thirteen, and, besides, I have had experience with Dr. Gilbert in New Orleans," I answered, trying to keep my voice in a polite tone.

"I was a boy, though, and you are just a girl," said Dr. Drake, as he looked down at me over the top of his glasses.

My heart was beating so fast and I was afraid I might let my temper get the better of me but I looked Dr. Drake in the eye, tried to ignore my fast beating heart, and said, "Dr. Drake, I thought you would be much smarter than that. You have worked with both men and women for a long time and I am sure that it has occurred to you that one is not necessarily smarter than the other but if you insist on keeping such ignorant assumptions, you may question me on my knowledge and see if it is not every bit the same as that of a young boy of thirteen who might have worked with Dr. Goforth."

As soon as I said that, I wanted to take the words right back; now I had put myself on trial and to the test.

Dr. Drake loved the challenge and he began firing questions at me.

"What do you prescribe for mild indigestion?"
"Red clover."

*"What would you recommended to someone
with poor circulation?"*
"Leaves of the fox glove plant."

"What is eczema?"
"A skin problem."

"What is the pancreas?"
"An organ in the body."

"Do you believe in bleeding the patient?"
"No, Sir."

For the next ten minutes Dr. Drake asked questions and I was able to answer every one. When the questioning was over Dr. Drake looked out the window and there was a long, uncomfortable silence in the room. I sat there not knowing if I should get up and leave or sit and stare or whether I was expected to say something.

Dr. Drake turned to me with a smile across his handsome face and said, "Littsie, you have a fine mind and a good aptitude for medicine. I think if you like long hours and you like people, you will be able to do the work. What do you think?"

"I am sure I can do the work," I said. I was so excited. "When would you like me to start and where and what time?"

"How about tomorrow, can you manage that?"

"Yes, yes, Sir," I answered.

And so, on weekends and holidays I would go to his office on Third Street and help out. It was what I enjoyed most and reminded me of my time in New Orleans with Doctor Gilbert. I cleaned the instruments, kept records of the patients and made the office presentable. But I also watched Dr. Drake as he worked and I learned so much from watching his skilled hands. And not just about people either, once in awhile he would work on animals too. As he said, "I was learning about man and beast."

Sometimes he would call me into the examining room and say, "Now watch this, Littsie. You may need to do this some day." And he would patiently show me how to fix a broken arm, or stitch a wound or remove a splinter, sometimes even a bullet. I loved watching him.

Every Saturday he would pay me one dollar for my work. I saved that money in a special place in my room. That money was very important to Megan and me. I had to take care of it.

"What about Euleen?" said Anne.

"Who is Euleen?" asked Johnnie.

"Don't you remember, Johnnie? Remember how Grandma told us that she was on a steamboat that helped another steamboat that had exploded. She pulled a slave girl from the river and hid her in her cabin. When they arrived in Cincinnati, Grandma Littsie was able to take her to Mr. Longworth's house. He saw to it that she was freed and did not have to be a slave anymore. I loved that part of your story, Grandma," said Isabelle. "Tell us about her."

Euleen lived and worked at the Longworth's house, I said. Mr. Longworth was one of the most important and richest men in the city. He was also one of the kindest. Whenever I had a few minutes of spare time I would walk over to the Longworth mansion to see Euleen. In order to get there I walked through the Fifth Street Market where people sold everything from fruits and vegetables to pigs and horses. Then I would walk along the public landing. It was always alive with steamboats and people arriving and leaving and wagons full of boxes to be shipped and goods being taken off boats that would soon be for sale in the city stores. As I walked, I heard bells, bells, bells. It was said then that Cincinnati had more bells than even New York. I could hear the steamboat horns and the click, clack of horses as their hoofs clattered on the cobblestone, the clink of hammers as another new building took shape and the calls of the vendors as they sold their goods from their wheelbarrows. And sometimes, if I timed it right, I might run into Mr. Foster. He worked as a bookkeeper in his brother's steamboat company. I don't think he really liked his job because I would often see him sitting outside playing his banjo and not doing his work. He loved music.

When I arrived at the Longworth House I would go to the back door and call for Euleen. It was not proper for a child to use the front door knocker.

"Oh, Euleen," I would call several times and after a few minutes a window would fly open and Euleen would call back.

"Be there in just a minute."

She would run to the back door and let me into the kitchen. Sometimes if I was lucky, Mr. Longworth's wife, Susan, would be there and she would always sit me down at the kitchen table and give me a slice of cake and a glass of milk to wash it down. Mrs. Longworth was raised when Fort Washington was still an important part of Cincinnati and she loved to tell stories of those early times.

"You're the little girl who helped Euleen, aren't you?" she asked one day. "You were awfully brave to bring her here."

"And you and Mr. Longworth were so good to make sure she got her freedom and did not have to be a slave anymore." I said.

"Perhaps," she said thoughtfully, "one day no one will have to be a slave."

Then she would tell Euleen and me to go out and have fun. And off we would go.

One particular time, oh, I remember it so well. The circus was in town and there was going to be a big parade. Megan and I met Euleen at the Longworth's kitchen and then headed to Fourth Street. We had never been to a circus. We did not have enough money to buy a ticket but we could watch the parade. That was free. We found a good spot near the front of the crowd and watched as the circus marched past. Oh, it was so wonderful. There were brightly painted wagons full of musicians. Lions rode in golden cages and roared so loud that Megan hid her face in my skirt. There were elephants in fancy dress, camels, monkeys, parrots, beautiful ladies on white horses, a man eating fire, and clowns, oh, so many clowns. We had never, ever seen anything like it. It was amazing. And then a group of acrobats came by walking on their hands, doing

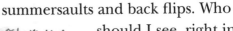

summersaults and back flips. Who should I see, right in the middle of them all, but my old friend and neighbor Tommy O'Brien. I had not seen him since I left Columbia during the cholera epidemic. And now here he was dressed in golden tights and a bright red jacket and doing cartwheels in a circus parade.

"Tommy," I yelled. "Tommy, over here."

He turned, surprised to hear his name, and when he saw me his broad Irish smile took over his whole face.

He ran across the street and gave me a big hug.

"Littsie, it is so good to see you. I thought we had lost you forever. Wherever have you been?"

"And I might ask you the same question, Tommy O'Brien. And look at you now, in the circus. Can you stay a minute or do you have to be in the parade?"

"No, no, it is alright, but just for a bit. I can join in again at the end."

I introduced him to Euleen and told him how we had met on a steamboat that exploded and how we were able to get Euleen freed from slavery. I had to introduce him to Megan, she had grown so much. And I told him how I had to search for so long to find her after we were separated when our parents died in the cholera epidemic. He told me about the hard times his family had gone through. He said joining the circus was the best thing he could do and, besides, it was fun and daring.

"Tommy, you have not changed since we roamed those hills in Columbia with Anne Belle Bailey. You were always doing something daring, you were an acrobat even then."

As we talked, the last of the circus began to roll by and Tommy fell in line in the back. As we joined him for a bit, we noticed that the horse we were following was lame and in pain.

"What is wrong with that horse?" I asked.

"Don't know," said Tommy. "Dan has been that way for a week. I am afraid that if he doesn't get better, he will be a goner. The circus won't keep a lame horse."

A gruff voice came from the last wagon, the one that carried the workers and the cooks, "He will be a goner as soon as this parade is over. I have orders to shoot him tonight. Can't pull around a lame horse."

"But," I said to Tommy, "maybe he can be helped."

"No helping this horse," the scruffy man said. "The only thing that will help him is the bullet."

"Have you tried......."

"Listen, girly," interrupted the man as he took a swig of something in a brown bottle, "t'aint your business and t'aint your horse. You run along now." His voice sounded familiar but I couldn't remember where I had heard it before. He wore his hat pulled low, covering his face, so I could not recognize him.

Strange, I thought, where have I heard that voice?

Turning my thoughts from the man in the wagon, I said "Sir, please let me take him. I will see what can be done."

"You are a pushy little girl," he said, as he staggered down off the wagon. "Why do I always run into pushy little girls? Listen here, Miss Smarty, I really don't care. You can take the blamed horse if you want to. He is good for nothing and it is one less piece of work that I will have to do today. Don't you dare bring him back. I don't want him in my way again."

Tommy gave me a look that said, "Don't say any more smarty things."

"Yes, Sir." I said softly as I took the horse by the bridle and held tightly.

The parade moved on and Euleen, Megan, Tommy and I stood at the end wondering what to do next. As we stood there it came back to me, I remembered the voice. It was the man who had come into my cabin on the steamboat when I was looking for Megan, the one who was looking for money, the mean one.

"That man," I said to Tommy. "Do you know him?"

"Only a little," said Tommy. "I try to stay away from him."

"I have had a run in with him once before," I said. "I am glad that he won't be in town long. Can't worry about him, right now we have to worry about Dan."

I looked up at the great big animal and knew immediately that we would be friends. He was a beautiful chestnut color with a full mane and a long bushy tail. His enormous legs had white feathered stockings. He was a draft horse used for pulling big loads and plowing farms. He had powerful shoulders and a long muscular neck. The circus used him to pull their wagonloads of equipment. You could tell that he was in pain; he tossed his head up and down and stood gingerly on his right front foot.

"We need to get him into a barn," I said.

"And just which barn do you think that might be?" asked Euleen.

"There is a barn behind Dr. Locke's school," I said. "It has not been used for much except storage. Let's take him there."

"I am sorry," said Tommy, "I have to get back for the show. It is almost time for my act. Look, I have grown very fond of Dan. I have a little extra money. Take it and buy him some food. It isn't much, but it will help. The circus will be moving on after the last show tonight. I don't know if I will be able to see you again. But good luck with Dan."

Tommy put the money in my hand and ran off toward the circus tents.

Food, I thought, as the circus music grew dimmer, how am I going to feed a big horse like Dan?

2
A PLACE FOR DAN

*T*HE barn behind our school was not large. It was just big enough for a few cows and maybe a horse or two. Even though it had not been used for several years, the smell of hay lingered. I was glad about that for there were still a few bales in the loft that would make Dan comfortable.

Megan, Euleen and I tied Dan to a post while we began to clean a stall for him. We swept it out, got the cob webs off the beams and cleaned the trough so we could fill it with fresh oats. We opened the window of the stall that looked out on the yard so that the sweet, fresh spring air could flow in. Megan found a bucket that we filled with water and then we covered the floor with hay. As we worked, Dan continued lifting his lame foot and tossing his head.

After we put him in the stall, he seemed a bit more relaxed and I began examining his legs and foot. His leg was tender to the touch and I had to be very gentle. I hope I can remember all Dr. Drake has taught me, I thought.

I lifted his hoof and examined it closely. It was red and swollen and looked infected. I looked closer and saw that there was the end of a splinter of wood in the infected area.

"I know how to get that out," I said. "I have watched Dr. Drake do that. All I need is a pair of pliers."

The three of us looked in all the boxes and shelves in the barn and found just what I needed. I took a deep breath and pulled at the splinter. It did not come out with the first try and Dan was getting more upset. I tried one more time and out it came. It was almost three inches long and caked with blood. No wonder the area was so red and swollen.

"I need to wash this and put some medicine on it," I announced.

"The washing part is easy," said Euleen. "What are you going to do about the medicine?"

Just then I heard a noise and looked up to see the sparkling blue eyes of Dr. Locke, our principal, looking in the barn door.

"Well, well, Littsie," he said. "I have been looking for you and so has Mrs. Craymore. She needs you to go to Mr. Proctor's store and buy some of his candles. We need them for the dinner table tonight."

"Oh, Dr. Locke," I said. "I am so glad you are here. Look what we have."

"My goodness, Littsie, that is one big

horse. Whose is it? Where did it come from?"

"Well, Sir, it is mine. I told the circus man I could help him. He didn't believe me and said to take him and not bring him back. He said that only a bullet would help him. I have taken care of his foot and now I need medicine but I don't have any," I said all in one breath.

"I have some medicine," he said. "I think you forgot that I teach pharmacy at the Medical College and that I am also a medical doctor. Megan, run tell Mrs. Craymore to give you the 'drawing out' bottle."

While Megan was gone Dr. Locke looked at Euleen and me and said, "And how do you think you are going to feed this big animal?"

"I have a little money that I have saved from working with Dr. Drake," I said.

"You need that for clothes for Megan," whispered Euleen.

"She certainly does," said Dr. Locke. "This is a beautiful animal. Does he have a name?"

"His name is Dan."

"Dan, you are one lucky horse to have Littsie as a friend," said Dr. Locke as he examined the swollen foot. "You did a good job here, Littsie. I think perhaps Dan is lucky for all of us. The school could use a horse for transportation and to pull some of the heavy loads we have. What do you say, Littsie? I will pay for the feed if you give Dan the care he needs."

"That sounds like a good deal," I said. "Just one problem. Will I still own the horse?"

"Of course," said Dr. Locke. "This is Littsie O'Donnell's horse."

Except for finding Megan I don't think I was ever so happy. Me, Littsie O'Donnell, with a horse of my own. I gave Dan a big hug and nuzzled his face. We were going to be good friends.

3
RETURN TO THE CABIN

WITH good care and good feed, Dan's foot healed quite nicely and he was able to do hard work for Dr. Locke and the school. I often wondered what the scruffy man from the circus would say if he could see him now. I did not want to meet up with him to find out.

I had not been to our family farm in Columbia since I left to look for Megan. I guess I had been afraid to go back; it held many good memories but many sad ones too. One afternoon, when the students were gone and Mrs. Craymore didn't need us, Megan and I saddled up Dan and headed for our little village, Columbia, about five miles away. It was easy for a big strong horse like Dan to carry both of us. Megan loved it and fit comfortably in front of me in the saddle.

We followed the river along the road that led east from downtown. We rode past the yards where steamboats were being built. I counted four of them along with saw mills and lumberyards. And there were new houses going up for the people who made these wonderous things. Steamboats were helping the city grow. They were the main way that people traveled now and many of them were made in Cincinnati. I loved to read their names: Patriot, Pioneer, Tecumseh, Ben Franklin, Queen of the West, Maid of Kentucky, names that all sounded so adventuresome.

We were almost to Columbia when the ground began to shake and I could hear a rumble, a rumble that was getting closer. Dan was beginning to fidget nervously. This was unusual for him as he was always calm and steady. I guided him to a spot off the road and Megan and I hopped out of the saddle and listened. From far away I could hear a whistle, a steam whistle like on steamboats and then I knew.

"Look, Megan, it is a train. I have heard of them but I have never seen one. Dr. Drake told me they were being built for Cincinnati."

And then I could see it as it rounded a bend. I could see the smoke stack with its great plume of steam and the huge steel wheels as they turned and pushed the heavy engine. The train's name was written on the side in great golden letters, *Little Miami Railroad*. It stopped near us and a man got out and inspected it all over. As Dan continued to fidget, I whispered to him gently and rubbed his head. That relaxed him a bit but he still was skittish.

The man was watching us and said, "Girls, today you are seeing history made. Trains will change things for all America, You mark my word. My name is Jacob Strader and I am part owner of this wonderful engine. Yes, yes, trains will change things. I own steamboats too, lots of them but these trains are what people will ride in the future."

Looking at Dan, he said, "You should be nervous, old boy. You won't have as many jobs to do. Trains will do all the heavy pulling now. And they will carry people too. In a few years stage coaches will be a thing of the past. You girls will ride trains, not horses, when you are my age."

I couldn't imagine a time without horses. They were everywhere, used for everything. I did not want to think of a time without Dan.

"Where does the train go?" I asked.

"Eventually it will go all the way to Springfield. We are still laying track for that and from there you will be able to connect to the Great Lakes. We are not quite ready yet, but it won't be long."

Dan was still not happy being so near that engine and the sound that it made, so I thought it best we be on our way.

"We need to get to Columbia, Mr. Strader," I said. "Good luck. I hope I get to ride your train some day."

"Oh, you will. You will," answered Mr. Strader as he waved to us from the engine's platform.

Dan was very happy to move on and carried us at a good pace right near to our farm. It had been two years since I had seen the farm and when it came into view I pulled Dan to a stop and almost froze. So many memories came rushing into my mind; Christmas with Papa and Mama, building the cabin, the closeness we felt on a cold winter night, the joy of the harvest, and the awful memories of when Mama and Papa got cholera and I had to go for medicine and, in the end, bury them.

Megan and I got off Dan and just stared at the

cabin. It was in terrible shape; several shingles had fallen off the roof, one of the posts on the porch was broken and some of the floor boards were missing. The door hung on only one hinge and vines had begun to grow up the sides and over parts of the roof. The fields that

Papa had worked so hard to farm were overgrown with briars and brush. The fence around the meadow was still in pretty good shape though, good enough to fence a horse. I took the saddle off Dan and led him into the pasture. I don't think he knew what to do with himself. He had never been let loose like this. At first he just stood there and pawed the ground but within a few minutes he was trotting around, stopping to nibble the grass and even rolling over on his back. He was glad to be free.

Megan and I held each others' hands and pushed in the creaking door of our cabin. The cabin was just as I had left it. There were still cooking pots at the fireplace, the table still had dishes set for supper, a book was on the seat of the rocking chair, blankets were left on the unmade beds and Megan's doll had fallen to the floor in a heap.

"Oh I remember her," she said, running to pick up the doll and give it a hug. "I got it for Christmas. Her name is Kate. Did you think I was never coming back, Kate? Don't worry, that is how I felt when Littsie was gone. But she did come back and now we are all together again."

I put my arms around her and said, "Yes, now we are all together again. And you and I have to keep on going. We have to do what Mama and Papa would want us to do. And I think one of the things they would want us to do is to clean up this cabin."

Megan looked at me with her big brown eyes and said, "Yes, let's do it."

"That's the O'Donnell way," I said.

We pulled the vines off the outside walls, opened the windows so that clean fresh air could come in, brought water from the well to wash the dishes and the pots and pans, scrubbed the floor, dusted everything and made the beds. I found Papa's hammer and fixed the hinge on the door and nailed the floorboards back down.

We neatly folded Mama and Papa's clothes and put them in the old trunk that we had brought from Pittsburg on the flatboat. When we opened the trunk we found a small blue velvet box. It held Mama's jewelry. She didn't have much but a few chains and two gold rings that Papa had given her. One ring had two entwined hands holding a heart and the other had some Irish words on it. When I examined it more closely I saw that it said "no anom cara."

"Oh, I remember these rings," I said. "Mama showed them to me when I was just a little girl like you, Megan. She only wore them at special times. Those Irish words mean, my soul friend."

"Do you think we can have them?" asked Megan.

"Yes, yes, I do," I said. "I know Mama would want us to have them. Here try this one on." Megan slid the one with the entwined hands on her tiny hands but it came right off. I tried the other one; it was just a bit loose.

"Tell you what," I said. "Let's see if we can put your ring on a chain that you can wear around your neck until your fingers get bigger." We searched and we did find a chain that worked well.

"Megan," I said, "these are O'Donnell rings. Whenever we are scared or tired or worrisome just give them a rub and think of Mama and Papa. They will help us. I know they will."

"Can't we stay here always?" asked Megan.

"I wish we could," I said. "Oh, how I wish. But I can't plow the fields like Papa or hunt or cut down trees or find the money to buy seed. And there is not a school for us here. Perhaps some day, when we are both older and stronger. Perhaps."

"We have to go back now, Megan," I said gently. "In a bit it will be dark and Mrs. Craymore will wonder where we are. We can come again and soon."

I brought Dan in from the pasture and saddled him. He was happy to come for he had had a good rest. We both climbed on his back and looked out over the valley towards the river and the soft rising hills. It was all so beautiful, so hard to leave. I rubbed my ring and nudged Dan and we headed back to Cincinnati. It had been a good day and we both felt better for going.

4
A BARN MEETING

AS we came closer to the city, we came to a large barn where people were gathering. Folks were coming from all directions and taking a seat on chairs and hay bales.

I was so curious I pulled Dan to a stop.

"Come on, Megan, let's see what is going on."

"But I am so tired, Littsie," she said

"Just for a little while, then we can go home," I said as I tied Dan to the hitching post with the other horses.

We went into the barn and took a seat in the back so as not to be noticed.

Pretty soon a powerful looking man stood on one of the bigger bales of hay and began to speak. He had dark curly hair and wore a shaggy brown linsey-woolsey suit and cowhide boots.

"Good evening, ladies and gentleman, and welcome to the Ohio Anti -Slavery Society," he said. "I am Theodore Weld and I am here tonight in hopes that you will join us in our fight against slavery."

"So that is it," I said to Megan. "I met some of these people in the market the other day. They were handing out pamphlets. They said they were abolitionists. They want to abolish slavery."

"What does abolish mean?" asked Megan.

"It means to do away with, get rid of," I said.

"There is nothing right about slavery," the speaker

went on. "It is all wrong. There is not any way that you can make it right. It is just plain wrong that one person can own another, that he can make him his property."

He spoke with a voice as powerful as thunder and in a manner that you wanted him to speak on and on.

"Let me tell you about slavery in the United States today," he said. "There are millions of people in slavery in our country. They, or their ancestors, were brought here in chains from Africa for the sole purpose of being sold as property so they could do someone else's work. They are poorly fed, poorly dressed, overworked and inhumanly punished. They are maimed, beaten, whipped and branded. Sometimes they have their ears cut off or their eyes knocked out. They are sold, separated from their families, made to walk in chains and to work in cotton fields far away."

"If that isn't enough suffering and torture, they are owned by someone else. Their bodies and their wives' bodies and their children's bodies are owned by another human being. How can that be in the land of the free? How can that be?"

As he spoke, I kept thinking of the first time I met Euleen. I kept thinking of the iron collar she had around her neck, of how she was owned by a man in Virginia, of how she had told me she was sold to him when she was only six and taken from her mother, of how she had no idea where her Mama or Papa were or if she even had any brothers or sisters. I thought of the slaves in chains getting off the boat that I had seen in New Orleans. I thought of the slaves I had seen across the river in Kentucky.

When Mr. Weld asked, in a booming voice, "Is there anything right about slavery?"

I answered with the rest of the crowd in a loud voice, "NO."

Megan had fallen asleep against my shoulder and stirred when the crowd roared its answer.

As Mr. Weld continued speaking, the sounds of sleigh bells, horns and drums could be heard from the back of the barn. People who did not like what he was saying, who wanted the country to keep having slaves, tried to drown him out so that he could not be heard.

"Don't let them bother us," said Mr. Weld. "They always try to silence me but I will not be silenced." And he kept on talking, his rich voice overcoming the noise. It was a battle between him and the noise makers. The bells and horns and drums eventually stopped because the people that had come to silence him had started to listen to what he had to say. They were now at least a little curious.

He turned to the crowd and said, "There is someone here I would like you to meet. Angelina Grimke is a friend of mine. Would you come forward, Angelina?"

A dark haired young woman came forward and said in a strong voice, "I am so happy to see all of you. I am the daughter of a slave owner. I was raised and cared for by slaves."

As she spoke the audience began to fidget and whisper to one another. A woman was never known to speak in public and they were astonished that Angelina Grimke was actually speaking.

"I am here to tell you that what Theodore Weld says is true. I grew up on a plantation that had over 100 slaves. I have seen it all. At the age of five I watched a slave whipped. That scene has stayed with me ever since. I have watched what slavery does to both the slave owner and the slave. I am here to tell you that it is not right and it must end." The audience clapped loudly as she sat down.

"Now," said Mr. Weld as he stood up again, "Will you help us? Will you join in the fight to end slavery? Will you stand up for what is right?"

At first no one answered and then all at once there was an answer as one,

"Yes, yes, we will." I was one of those who said yes.

"All right, all right." he said. "Over there is Levi Coffin and John Rankin and James Birney. Speak to them. They will tell you how you can help. We cannot rest until there is no more slavery in the United States of America."

"And now, thank you for coming tonight and for your help."

The audience gave him a standing ovation. There was a feeling of hope and energy in the air, a feeling that all of us, working together, could bring slavery to an end.

I couldn't talk to any of the people Mr. Weld mentioned that night. Megan was so tired, I needed to get her to bed. I will look for Mr. Birney tomorrow, I said to myself.

"Wake up, Megan," I said. "We must go. It is dark and it will be hard for Dan to find his way home."

As we came out of the barn, something hit Megan in the back of the head and she cried out. I turned and saw that it was an egg, a rotten, very old and smelly egg. It was oozing through her hair and down her face. And then I realized that many people were being hit with rotten eggs. Friends of the people who had made all the noise in the meeting were the ones throwing the eggs.

"Get out of here you darky lovers. You love to make trouble, don't you? You are just like thieves, trying to take my property. You are rotten scum," they shouted. One voice mingled with the others and stood out. Could it be the nasty man from the circus or was I imagining it? I listened closely, I was sure it was him. I have to get Megan out of here, I thought. I don't want her to be where he is.

A voice behind me said, "Act like it doesn't bother you, Miss. It makes them happy to see you get upset."

We quickly moved towards Dan but when we got to the hitching post we saw that all the horses' manes and tails had been clipped very short. Dan's beautiful full tail and his gorgeous mane were just stubs. He looked upset and was snorting and whining.

"They are at it again," someone said. "They did this at the last meeting too. Now everyone knows us as abolitionists when we ride our horses. Let the whole world know how we feel. I, for one, am proud of it. Clip away, boys."

I was so angry. "How can you let them throw rotten eggs and clip the most beautiful part of your horse? Do you just let them do it?" I shouted. "Look at your horse. He looks terrible."

"We don't believe in violence, young lady. We will report it to the sheriff but he probably won't do anything about it because just across the river slavery is legal. You see it is harder to be an abolitionist than just saying "yes" at a meeting. You have to be really determined and willing to take what comes."

My thoughts were tumbling over one another. Megan was crying, my horse was snorting, more rotten eggs were flying and that voice was still yelling. To be an abolitionist is very serious business, I thought. Perhaps it is just for grown ups, perhaps I am too young. And then I thought of Euleen and her family and I knew that serious or not I had to be an abolitionist.

5
THE RIGHT THING

*T*HE very next day I rode Dan proudly through the city, his clipped mane and tail were badges of honor and I noticed other horses that had also been clipped. I was glad to be riding one of them. I found Euleen and told her all that had taken place the night before. She was very excited.

"Do you mean all those folk really want to end slavery? They really want my family not to be enslaved?"

"Yes, yes, Euleen, and we can help. All we have to do is talk to Mr. Birney."

"Let's go right now," she said.

His office was not far. We found him busy at his desk writing for the next edition of his newspaper, *The Philanthropist.* He was a big man with a kindly face and a ready smile.

"Mr. Birney," I said as we approached his desk, "I am Littsie O'Donnell and this is Euleen Randolph. I was at the meeting of the Ohio Anti- Slavery Society last night. Mr. Weld said to talk to you if we wanted to help."

Mr. Birney looked at Euleen. "Are you a freed slave, child?" he asked gently.

"Yes, Sir, Mr. Longworth saw to that."

"I am glad because it can be dangerous for escaped slaves that have not been legally freed. As you know, Ohio is a free state, slavery is not allowed here. But if a slave escapes and comes here, his master has the right to come and take him back because he is his property. It is better for the slave to keep going north. If he is lucky, he will make it to Canada. Slave catchers are not allowed there."

"How do they do that?" I asked. "It would be so hard."

"That is where we come in," he said. "Those of us who want to help, guide escaped slaves to a safe place and then to another safe place until they are far away from the slave catcher. This system is called The Underground Railroad and people who help are called conductors. You see it is not really a railroad but a system of people helping escaped slaves."

"Are there many conductors?" I asked.

"Yes, but they must be quiet about it because they could be put in jail for helping a slave. I wish we could end all slavery tomorrow. I am the son of slave owners. I actually received slaves as a wedding gift but when I saw how evil slavery was I freed them all and began to work to set all slaves free. Not everyone agrees though, just look at this."

Mr. Birney handed me a copy of the *Cincinnati Daily Post.* The article was about abolitionists and it said, "If any of their authors or agents should be found here, LYNCH THEM."

"That's me they are talking about, I am an abolition author," said Mr. Birney. "They would like to see me hung. This is dangerous business, Littsie, and you girls are awfully young. What do your parents say?"

"My parents died in the cholera epidemic," I answered.

"And mine are still enslaved. I have no idea where they are," added Euleen.

I could see the sympathy on Mr. Birney's face, as he said, "I am so sorry for both of you. I know it must be hard."

He sat thinking for a few minutes and then said, "You know, sometimes your youth would be an advantage. Not many people would suspect you."

Until they look at my horse, I thought.

"I can't guarantee that you won't be hurt," continued Mr. Birney. "Do you still want to help?"

I rubbed Mama's ring, took a deep breath and looked at Euleen. "Yes, Sir," we both said together.

"All right then," he said. "We will see what you can do tonight. We almost always work at night because we can't take the chance of being seen during the day. We have word that a young slave woman from Kentucky will try to cross the river tonight near the far end of the public landing. You must find her and lead her to the

Dumas House Hotel. Do you know where that is?"

"Yes, Sir," Euleen said. "It is on Eastern Row. I have seen a lot of black folks there."

"They will help her get to the next safe place," said Mr. Birney. "Be careful now and be quiet too. No one must know what you are doing."

"How do we know we have the right people?"

"The password is *The Boatman Dance.* Remember that."

I smiled and thought that is the song that my family sang when we came down the river on a flatboat. It is the one that Megan was singing when I found her at the Cincinnati Orphan Asylum. It helped us, maybe it will help other folks.

Euleen and I looked at each other and shook hands. "I will see you tonight at the Public Landing at 8:00. Don't be late," said Euleen.

"You are brave girls," said Mr. Birney. "You are doing what is right, don't ever forget that. Goodbye now and good luck," he said.

That night after I finished my chores for Mrs. Craymore and got Megan tucked in bed, I quietly slipped out the door and made my way to the river. The bustling daytime landing was settling down for the night. Steamboat passengers were sitting at dinner in quiet candle lit dining rooms. Workers on the boats, finished with their work for the day, were resting on cotton bales or sitting around playing cards. In the distance I could hear Mr. Foster playing his banjo and I could also hear the beating of my heart. I can't tell you that I was not afraid.

Euleen came running up. "I thought I would never get out of the Longworth kitchen tonight. They had so many guests. That always makes more work."

"Are you scared?" I asked.

"Of course," said Euleen.

"Me too!"

We walked slowly across the public landing, staying in the shadows of the buildings so that we wouldn't be noticed, keeping absolutely silent. As we got further away from the boats, we found an area by the river filled with trees and bushes. We chose that as a hiding spot. Clouds had hidden the light of the moon. The river's water lapped quietly on the shore. I remembered an Irish prayer that my mother used to say when she was afraid:

> *Be Thou between me and all things grisley,*
> *Be Thou between me and all things mean,*
> *Be Thou between me and all things gruesome*
> *Come with me.*

I whispered it and gave Mama's ring a rub. Presently we heard the sound of oars in the river and saw a boat approaching over the dark waters. A black man got out and pulled the boat up on the shore and then helped a young woman out of the boat. Euleen and I came forward from the bushes and when the man saw us he whispered, "Do you have words?"

"*The Boatman Dance*," Euleen whispered.

"My name is William Casey. A bit young, aren't you?" he asked.

"People don't suspect young ones," I said.

He chuckled a bit and said, "I guess you are right about that."

Then, turning to the woman, he said. "She needs care. She is weak and hungry. Hasn't had much food in two days and has been running barefoot from dogs the whole time. It is good we got her when we did. I don't know how much longer she could have gone on. Quickly now, take her to the back door of the Dumas House. You younguns be careful now."

When I looked at the woman I saw what Mr. Casey meant. Her clothes were all in tatters and her feet were bleeding. Her face was swollen and blood ran down her cheek. She was so weak she could not speak.

"This way," Euleen said to her gently.

I put my arm around her and we slowly retraced our steps through the Public Landing to the Dumas House. Several times we had to stop just so she could rest a bit. Fortunately, there were not many people on the streets and we made it to the back door of the Dumas House undetected.

I knocked softly at the door and a young man answered. He looked at us silently and I said, "The Boatman Dance." He nodded, opened the door and took the woman inside. I knew she would be taken care of.

Euleen and I smiled at each other. "We did it," she said. "We younguns did it. I think we can do this again."

"We sure can," I said. "But tonight we must get back before we are missed."

From then on Euleen and I helped escaping slaves whenever Mr. Birney asked us. Mrs. Craymore was happy to watch Megan for me. I couldn't tell her what I was doing but I think she knew somehow and that she approved. I couldn't tell Megan either. She was at the age when she couldn't keep secrets and I couldn't risk it.

"I can keep a secret," said Andrew, as he reached for another cookie.

"Stop interrupting Grandma Littsie" said Isabelle.

"Go on, Grandma."

Well, we met slaves in different places. Sometimes
they just walked off the steamboats where they had been
working, sometimes they came to Cincinnati with their
masters from Kentucky to do business and they would
wander off, very often they crossed the river at night.
We would lead them to different places too; sometimes
to the Mill Creek, sometimes to College Hill, sometimes
to the homes of Salmon Chase or Gamaliel Bailey or
Tom Duram and sometimes to churches. Each one
would help them move on to someone else until they
finally got to Canada.

There were people in Cincinnati who helped in
other ways too. There was a group of women who sewed
clothes for escaping slaves. When slaves arrived in
Cincinnati they were usually in the rags that they wore
on the plantation. Slave catchers always looked for that.
These women sewed clothes for the escaped slaves so
that they would look like everyone else and not be so
noticeable. Other people provided food. Dr. Drake
often took care of their medical needs. More than once
I saw his sorrow when he treated the back of a slave that
had been whipped. Salmon Chase provided free legal
work and William Watson made sure they had proper
hair cuts.

And Dan. What a help he was! We would take him
when there were more than two people and we would
need a wagon. Sometimes we covered his hoofs with
burlap so that you couldn't hear the sound of his hoofs

on the cobblestones. He seemed to know what was going on because he would keep very quiet and never snort or whinny. He could carry three people on his back without any trouble.

And Tommy O'Brien helped too.

"I thought Tommy was in the circus," said Andrew.

He was for awhile, then one day I saw him in the market doing back flips and hand springs and a crowd had gathered to watch. After he gave his performance he passed his hat around for coins. When he finished his act and I got his attention, he told me that the owner of the circus refused to pay him and he needed money to eat, so he left and came back to Cincinnati. "I am doing okay," he said. "I could do better though."

I told him about the Underground Railroad and took him to see Dan. Tommy was pleased to see his old friend in such good shape. His tail and mane had grown back and he was a most handsome horse now.

Tommy wanted to know more about the Underground Railroad. "Littsie, when you go to the landing aren't you afraid you will be noticed?" he asked.

"When it is dark and there are not many people, it is not so bad. But when there are lots of folks there, I do get a little scared," I said. I couldn't admit that I got really, really scared.

"I have an idea," he said. "Tell me when you are going and I can come and draw the crowd for my show and you can sneak around behind them."

"It was a great idea and we used it often. So you see

that is how Tommy O'Brien, the circus acrobat, helped,"
I said to Andrew.

"Keep going, Grandma," said Isabelle. "Don't stop."

"Yes, Yes. Now where was I? Now I remember."

We were always looking out for the slave catchers
that the masters hired to bring back their slaves. We
learned to spot them pretty easily. They were rough and
mean and always armed. Actually, Euleen and I were
very proud of ourselves; not many that we helped got
caught by the slave catcher. There were a few though
and it broke my heart to see them taken in chains on
to a steamboat to be taken back to the plantation
and slavery.

6
UPSETTING CHANGES

ONE day at school Dr. Locke came to the students while we were eating lunch and said that after lunch we were to gather outside for a special announcement. We were all excited thinking that we were going to have a picnic or maybe even a free day. But it was none of those things.

When we were all together Dr. Locke stood up and said, "My dear students it is with a heavy heart that I speak to you today. I love this school and all that goes on here but I have been offered a position as a professor at the Medical School of Ohio and I have accepted it. That means that I will have to close the school for I cannot do both. I hope all of you understand. There are several other schools in the city and I will be happy to supply them with your records. We have had good and productive years here and I have enjoyed every minute of it. But I must move on. I wish you much good luck and good studies in the future."

I was stunned, more than stunned. What was I going to do now? Where would Megan and I live? How would we eat? How could we pay for school? My few hours with Dr. Drake would not pay for all that. We couldn't go back to the farm. I knew very little about farming. I just knew a little bit about medicine. It would be a long time before I knew enough to make a living from it. And what about Dan?

I heard the other girls talking. Julia Burnet said that she would be going to Mr. Picket's school, Amanda Drake said that she had a friend at the Ryland School and that she liked it a lot. Eliza Longworth said that her parents knew Miss Harriet Beecher and her sister Catherine. They ran a school called the Western Female Institute. All of this was so confusing. I had heard that some schools, called common schools, had been started in Cincinnnati, and you did not have to pay tuition. That would help, but where would we live, and how could we pay rent?

Perhaps I could find the same kind of situation that I had here at Dr. Locke's at another school, I thought. At least Mrs. Craymore and Dr. Locke would say that I was a good worker and a good student. I was sure that they would write a recommendation for me. Megan was coming along too. She was almost seven now and had learned to read. She was able to lend a hand in the kitchen drying dishes and sweeping up. And of course, whomever I lived with had to be on the side of the Underground Railroad.

That next day Megan and I made our way over to the Mr. Chute's School. As we were coming up the walk, I recognized several girls from my class. They were full of excitement and stopped to tell me that this is where they would be going to school.

"You come too, Littsie," they said, "it will be fun."

They did not know how complicated it was going to be for me. They did not know that I did not have any tuition money.

I rang the bell and a tall woman with glasses on the end of her nose answered.

"Good day," she said. "May I help you?"

"I hope so," I said. "You see, my sister and I were students at Dr. Locke's school and now it is closing and I was wondering if you would have a place for us here."

"Come this way," she said and she led us into a small office.

"Now let me see, you are fourteen and your sister is seven. Well we do have two places left but they are the last two. So many of the girls from Dr. Locke's school are coming here. The tuition for you both will be $80.00. Tell your parents to bring the money tomorrow and you can start next week."

"That is the problem," I said quietly. "Megan and I lost our parents in the cholera epidemic. When we went to Dr. Locke's school he let us work around the school and stay there instead of paying tuition. I have a note here from him. He highly recommends us."

"And he let us keep Dan in the barn," Megan interrupted.

"Dan in the barn? Is he your brother?"

"No," laughed Megan, "he is our horse. He is very beautiful."

The lady was not at all friendly. When she spoke to us she looked down over her glasses without a smile. Mama's prayer came back to me again and it made me giggle inside.

Be Thou between me and all things grisley,
Be Thou between me and all things mean,
Be Thou between me and all things gruesome,
Come with me.

"Well then," she said, "there is no room here for the likes of you. We are not a boarding school and we don't keep our students' horses. We must have tuition money before any student begins. I suggest you look elsewhere," and she quickly showed us the way to the door and slammed it as we left.

It had begun to rain and as we walked down the steps, raindrops mixed with the bitter tears that flowed down my cheeks. I had tried so hard for so long to take care of the two of us and I had never cried. But that nasty woman made me feel so low and unworthy that all the tears I had held back ever since that awful day in Columbia when Papa and Mama died came pouring out in one great wave of sorrow.

Megan looked up at me surprised and a little frightened by my tears. "Don't cry, Littsie," she said putting her little arms around me. "We will find a way. I know we will." She pulled on Mama's ring that she wore around her neck and said, "We are O'Donnells, remember?"

It made me smile to hear Megan talk like that, such a wise little girl. I gave her a hug and dried my tears and said, "Yes, we are O'Donnells and we will find a way, for sure."

"What about that Western Female Intute, that the other girls were talking about?"

"Institute." I corrected her. "I think it is run by Miss Beecher and her sister. They live at the edge of the city almost two miles from here," I said.

"We have Dan," she said. "He will take us."

"Of course," I said. "Let's go get him."

7
A NEW HOME

SUMMER was just beginning and as Dan carried us up the hill from the city towards the area called Walnut Hills, we could smell the summer woodland flowers and the sweet scent of the black locust tree. The sun on our backs felt good after the long cold winter. The muddy road was full of ruts but Dan's gentle stride made the ride pleasurable and the bad feelings we carried from the nasty lady melted into the vast expanse of blue sky that surrounded us.

Soon we were standing before the home of Miss Harriet Beecher. It was an inviting building that sat back a bit from the road at the edge of the forest. Nearby was the Lane Seminary where Miss Beecher's father taught. I jumped down out of the saddle and held the reins so that Megan could get down too. We stood at the bottom of the stone steps and looked at each other.

"Remember we are O'Donnell's," we both said at once and then we held hands and walked up the steps and across the porch and knocked on the door. As we waited for someone to answer, we could hear the sound of laughter and merriment inside. I took that as a good sign.

A tall gentle woman opened the door and I held my breath a moment hoping that I would not need Mama's prayer again.

"Yes," she said. "Is there something I can do for you?"

"We have heard that there is a school for girls here," we answered.

"Oh, I am afraid you are mistaken, the school is located in the city at 4th and Sycamore but do come inside. You look like you could use a bit of lemonade. My name is Miss Dutton. And you are?"

"Littsie and Megan O'Donnell," I answered.

"What a nice name. I knew some O'Donnells back east," she said, leading us into the house.

As we went inside, we could hear noise tumbling from the kitchen and the sound of a fiddle.

"You will find this to be a very busy and unusual house," she said. And with that an older man came through the parlor playing a fiddle and dancing in his bare feet, followed by giggling children.

"I guess you can see what I mean," said Miss Dutton. "That is Dr. Lyman Beecher. He is a preacher and he does love that fiddle and so do the children."

She led us into the kitchen where we found several women cooking. "This is Aunt Esther and one of the servants, Mina. And this is my good friend Harriet Beecher."

"These girls are interested in our school," Miss Dutton said to Miss Beecher. "This is Littsie O'Donnell and this is Megan O'Donnell."

Megan and I each turned to Miss Beecher and said, "Pleased to meet you, Ma'am."

Miss Beecher was seated at the kitchen table surrounded by pen and paper, a rolling pin, ginger, flour, eggs and various cooking utensils. She was a small woman with brown hair and blue-gray eyes. She was trying to write but kept being distracted by what was going on in the kitchen. She looked up and with a kindly smile said, "It is very nice to meet you girls. 'Littsie' what a pretty name that is, unusual. Mina, could you check the ginger bread cookies and ask father please not to play the fiddle so long. Where is the inkstand?"

"On top of the tea kettle," answered Mina.

And then, quickly turning to us, Miss Beecher said, "And what brings you to us?"

"Well Ma'am, I said, "you see we attended Dr. Locke's school but it is closing and we must find another school."

"I think you could come to the Western Female Institute," she said as she continued writing.

"But that is not all of the problem," I said. "You see our parents died in the cholera epidemic and we have been able to live at Dr. Locke's school because we work in the kitchen and such. I have a note from him if you would like to see it. And sometimes I work with Dr. Drake."

Miss Beecher stood up and quickly walked to the lemonade, poured two glasses, gave them to us and put her arms around me. She had made up her mind. She did not need to ask more questions.

"Of course, you can come to our school. You have had trouble enough. We must work something out. I am afraid though that this house is full. There are thirteen of us here. I don't think there is a spot for you."

All the time Miss Beecher was talking, Megan was pulling at my skirt.

"Don't forget to tell her about Dan."

"Miss Beecher," I said, "There are a few other things I should tell."

"Yes, go on," she said, as if she had always heard complications.

"We have a horse, a very nice horse. His name is Dan. He was a circus horse and can do lots of work."

" A horse!" she smiled with delight. "A horse that can pull heavy loads?"

"Yes," I answered with a little hesitation, afraid to be hopeful.

"Oh my, could we use a horse," she said with glee. "We are a bit low on money now and we can't buy one. If I sell more of my writings, the situation could improve. Your horse would certainly help us out. What we do have is a barn and, come to think of it, there is a small room attached in the back where you and your sister could stay. It will be cold in the winter but we will pile you with blankets and try to stuff the cracks. You can wear nightcaps and mittens to bed. And of course with all this land at the edge of the forest, we do have a pasture for Dan. Am I right? Is that your horse's name?"

"Yes, Ma'am," I said. "Dan would love a pasture. He has never had one."

"But there is one other problem," I said. "Sometimes we may need Dan because," I said with caution, "I do some work for Mr. Birney."

"Mr. Birney, who writes *The Philanthropist?*"

"Yes," I said, thinking I may have just said the wrong thing.

She jumped right up and said. "Hurrah for you!" and she gave me a big hug. "You have come to the right place. Any friend of James Birney is a friend of mine. Yes, yes. You will stay here and go to our school. Now you show me Dan and I will show you the barn."

I brought Dan around to the back of the house and followed Miss Beecher to the barn. She was delighted with my beautiful horse and he took to her right away. As we entered the barn, swallows that nested in the loft sang their hellos and the sweet smell of fresh hay wrapped around us. Dan's stall was clean and fresh and right next to the family cow, Bossie.

Our room at the back was not quite as nice as our room at Dr. Locke's but it was large enough and we could make it comfortable. And now, in the summer, with the big barn door open, breezes floated in and

cooled the animal stalls and our room as well. Miss
Beecher managed to find us a bed and boxes for the few
things that we carried. She hammered pegs into the
walls so that we would have somewhere to hang our
clothes. Between the studs, she hung some shelves and
said "These will be for your books."

"I am afraid that we don't have any books," I
said softly.

"No books? How can a child not have any books?
Impossible!"

"Books are very expensive," I said in a whisper. "We
don't have money for them."

"Well, we shall fix that and we will fix it right now."

Miss Beecher took me by the hand and led us back
to the house and into her father's study. The room was
filled with books: books that rose from the floor right up
to the ceiling, books tall and short, books of every color.
The room held the captivating smell of leather bindings
and new paper. I had never seen so many books in my
whole life. It was magical. I wanted to stay there and
read every one of them.

"I have always thought that books have friendly
quiet faces," she said. "Just look at them now, all inviting
you to get to know them. And you are welcome to
borrow any of them. That small bookcase under the
window holds my favorites. They are all by Sir Walter
Scott; *Ivanhoe, Rob Roy, The Pirate* and many more. You
must read them."

"May I borrow those as well?" I asked.

"Of course you can, anytime."

Miss Harriet then took us to a stack of books on the floor and said, "Here is your first, very own book" and she handed us each a lovely book. "It is a book that I wrote, *Primary Geography for Children*."

"A geography book," I said with delight. "I love to read about far away places."

"I don't think I can read this yet," said Megan.

"You will be able to soon," I said "when we start school again."

That night after dinner and after helping in the kitchen, we snuggled into our new bed in the barn and I read *Primary Geography for Children* out loud to Megan by the light of the moon. We read about far away places with strange sounding names: Ethiopia, Zanzibar, Mozambique and Angola. We read about the people and the plants and the oceans. And while we read, we could hear the soft sound of Dan's breathing, Bossie's tail hitting the sides of the stall, a cat getting comfortable for the night and, somewhere outside, the hoot of an owl. I rubbed Mama's ring and knew once again that she and Papa were somehow with us.

8
A SPECIAL PAINTER

*T*HE following week I brought Dan in from his new pasture, saddled him up, rode the two miles to the city, and made my way to the Longworth House to see Euleen. I wanted to tell her all that had happened and let her know where we were living. As I approached the house from the back, where the servants' door was located, I found Euleen talking with a young man in house painter's clothing.

"Littsie," she called, "Come here. I want you to meet someone. This is Robert Duncanson."

"How do you do," I said. The young man turned with a brush in his hand and smiled. He was about my age, tall and good looking.

"What brings you to Cincinnati?" I asked.

"Relatives," he said. "I am here with my mother for the summer. We are from Michigan and from Canada too."

"Two places at once?" I asked.

"I go to Canada to school. My father thinks it is much better especially for the son of a freed slave."

"Yes, I have a problem with schools too," said Euleen. "I can't go to school with white children, even friends like Littsie. Mr. Longworth has given money for a school for colored children. That is where I go. I have learned a lot but it feels funny knowing that we all can't go to the same school."

My heart broke when she said this. We were such good friends. It just wasn't right that we couldn't go to the same school. I didn't know what to say.

"Littsie," she said, "Robert not only paints houses, he paints beautiful pictures. Just look." She turned to some paintings stacked against the wall. They were beautiful. Most of them were pictures of nature but there were a few portraits as well.

"They are lovely," I said.

"I need to learn more," he said quietly. "There is so much more that I need to know. Have you ever heard of John James Audubon. Now there is a painter. Someone told me that he spent some time in Cincinnati. He draws things from nature, especially birds."

"I think Mr. Longworth has something like that," said Euleen. "I have seen it in the parlor."

"Do you think you could show it to us?" asked Robert.

"Well, we can give a try," Euleen answered. "But we must be quiet."

Robert and I followed as Euleen led us through the kitchen and up the stairs, past rooms full of beautiful furniture, velvet drapes and soft carpets, to a small parlor off the front hall. There, hung on the wall over the fireplace, was a painting of an eagle. It was so lifelike, as if it had just flown in the window. The eagle was powerful and strong and majestic. In the background were glistening snowcapped mountains. It was beautiful.

Robert did not say anything. He just looked and

looked and looked some more.

And then a deep voice said, "So you like the painting, do you?"

I jumped a little and turned to see Mr. Longworth in his old gardening clothes standing in the doorway.

"Yes, Sir, I certainly do," said Robert. "Mr. Audubon is a master."

"I bought that from him when he was living in Cincinnati," said Mr. Longworth. "I think he lives in New Orleans now. And you are right, he is a master."

"Robert paints pictures too, Mr. Longworth," said Euleen.

"Aren't you painting my house?" asked Mr. Longworth.

"Yes, Sir, but I also paint pictures."

"Do you have any with you? I would like to see them."

"I would be glad to show them to you," said Robert and he led the way to the back yard.

Mr. Longworth looked through the stack carefully and thoughtfully.

"These are quite good, in fact very good. I would like to buy a few of them from you now. Do you live around here?"

"No Sir, I am just visiting for the summer."

"I'll tell you what. If you are here next summer and you are still interested in painting, come and see me. Perhaps we can work something out."

Robert smiled his handsome smile. "Yes, Sir," he said, and extended his hand to shake Mr. Longworth's. "Yes, Sir. That sounds good to me."

"You can count on Mr. Longworth," said Euleen. "I should know. He gave me my freedom."

Mr. Longworth smiled gently at Euleen and then as he went back into the house he turned and said, "You have talent, young man. Yes, you do."

"By golly, I am for sure coming back to Cincinnati," said Robert.

"You better, we will all be looking for you," said Euleen. Then turning to me she said, "What brings you here today, Littsie?"

"Well," I said, "I guess you heard that Dr. Locke's school is closing. I just wanted to let you know that Megan and I are staying at the Beecher home. Well not exactly in the home. We are in a room in the barn with Dan. It is cozy and comfortable though. Miss Beecher said that we could go to the Western Female Institute. Of course, we will be working at the school and at their house and I will continue to work for Dr. Drake. I tell you though, Euleen, that house is a jolly one. There are thirteen people there and there is always something happening. And, they are friends with Mr. Birney. That helps a lot. You must come for a visit."

"I sure will," she said.

And she did. That summer was one to remember for both of us. The dreaded cholera did not return to the city and for some reason our chores and duties were light. Dr. Drake had gone out of town for a few months, so I was not needed there. For the first time in a long time we had time to play. Very often some of the younger Beecher children would come with us and sometimes Tommy O'Brien would come too. We taught them how to look for crawdads in the streams and how to cook the cattail plant just like Anne Belle Bailey taught us. We climbed high in the loft of the barn and swung on a rope right out the barn door. That was scary and made our tummies do flip flops but we loved it.

On hot days we would go for a swim in the creek. It was so lovely to be squeaky clean on a summer day. You know we couldn't take a bath very often then so being able to swim in the creek was a treat. Afterwards we would gather wild strawberries and eat them as we lay on our backs among the daises and watched clouds as they decorated the blue, blue sky of summer. We explored all the woods that surrounded the Beecher's house. Some days we would ride Dan to the bluff that overlooked the city and the river. It was so beautiful there with all the soft rising hills bordering the river. You could see the steamboats docked at the public landing and all the different kinds of boats on the river: flatboats, rowboats, sailboats, ferry boats, canoes and rafts. You could see the tiny villages across the river in Kentucky and the farms that bordered them. But each time that I looked at this beautiful scene, I thought how sad it was that one side of the river had slavery and one did not.

"I wish I could have been there," said young Andrew.

"Oh, you have your kind of fun," I said. "But I do want to tell you about one funny thing in particular. Do you remember how I told you that pigs roamed the streets of Cincinnati?"

"Yes, yes," they answered.

They were all over the place and I must say they were pretty nasty. They would push you aside just to get to a small piece of garbage. One day I was in the Beecher's garden gathering apples from the small orchard that lay at the back of the house. I looked up to see Tommy O'Brien coming toward me riding a PIG. Really, he was riding a big, white pig. Megan saw him from our room behind the barn and came running with peals of laughter. Just then another pig pushed his way into the yard.

"Get up on that one and we can have a race," said Tommy to Megan.

Megan did not need to be asked twice and with Tommy's

help she was quickly on top of the pig. Tommy and
Megan raced round and round the orchard on those
pigs. The pigs themselves seemed to enjoy the fun, you
know they are awfully smart. That was some day, the pig
racing day.

"Yuck, I don't think I would like to sit on a nasty
pig," said Isabelle. "It would be all muddy and smelly. I
am glad that happened long ago."

"Tell some more," Andrew said. "I love your
stories, Grandma."

"You're sure you want more?" I asked.

"More and more and more," they all chanted

Well, as I remember the house had many visitors
that summer: Uncle Samuel and Aunt Elizabeth Foote,
Salmon Chase, Mr. Longworth and his wife, Susan, and
even Mr. Birney. The one that I loved to listen to most
was Reverend John Rankin. He was a tall, good looking
man. He always had an armful of stories and many of
them were about the Underground Railroad. He lived in
Ripley about fifty miles from Cincinnati. He had a house
at the top of a hill where he would hide slaves who had
escaped from their masters and had crossed the river,
seeking freedom. He and his wife and children would
give them food and shelter and then guide them to the
next house that would do the same until they got to
Canada where the slave catcher could not come. When
Reverend Rankin came to Cincinnati he would make it a
point to stop by the Beechers' home. There was always
lively conversation and it was most interesting just to

listen. I will never forget one of the stories he told.

One extremely cold night in March of the previous year he, had just lit the freedom lamp and put it in the window.

"What is a freedom lamp?" asked Anne.

It was a light that people who helped in the Underground Railroad put in their window so that escaping slaves would know that this was a safe house and the people who lived there would help them.

Anyway, he had just lit the lamp and put it in the window not an hour before, when there was a very soft knock on the door. He opened the door to find a young slave woman holding a baby. She was wet and shivering, her feet were bleeding and she was very frightened. Reverend Rankin quickly took her indoors. While his wife helped her get warm, gave her food and took care of the baby, the woman told her story. She had escaped from a very mean mistress and ran through the woods to the river. As she ran she could hear the sound of the master's dogs barking as they chased her. When she got to the river she could see that it had turned to ice but that the ice was beginning to melt. She could also see the light in John Rankin's window and knew that there was hope. There was no turning back now for her and she was determined that her baby would not grow up in slavery. She jumped onto the first patch of ice in her bare feet and held her baby tightly. As the ice began to sink she jumped onto the next patch but this time she slipped and she had to put the baby on the ice and pull herself out of the water. She kept looking at that tiny flickering light and she made herself go on. Finally she made it to the shore and followed the path up the hill to the light. Now in the care of the Rankins, she let her exhaustion take over and her body relax. Miraculously, the baby was not crying but was sound asleep. Reverend and Mrs. Rankin quickly got her ready to move to the next house for they knew that the slave catchers would not be far behind. And the plan worked. Reverend Rankin had just recently heard that she did make it to Canada and was doing quite well there.

The children were very quiet after that story, just like I was the first time I heard it.

"Do you think that there were many people that had that dangerous of an escape?" Johnnie asked.

" Yes, many," I said. "maybe not on the ice, but in many different dangerous ways."

"They must have been so brave," said Isabelle.

"Yes, indeed they were," I answered. "They were seeking freedom and very often those who are seeking freedom have to be very brave."

Oh, yes, towards the beginning of fall a man named Calvin Stowe began to come to the Beecher house more and more often. I would see him with Miss Beecher when they went to church or to the Semi-Colon Club. I began to think they were sweet on each other.

"What does sweet on each other mean?" asked Andrew.

"Don't you know, silly?" asked Isabelle. "It means they *looove* each other."

"Mush," said Andrew. "Get to the good part."

We started school at the Western Female Institute that fall. Miss Dutton, Miss Harriet and Miss Tappan were our teachers. Miss Catherine, Miss Harriet's sister, was the principal. Everything seemed to fall into place for both Megan and me. We were able to continue where we left off at Dr. Locke's and even some of my friends from Dr. Locke's were in my class. Our days were long and full. Up at 5:00 am to dress, give Dan his oats and clean his stall, milk Bossie and turn her out into the pasture and then hurry with the milk over to the house to help Mina get breakfast going for all 15 people. That meant getting the woodfire going, setting the table, kneading the dough for biscuits, frying bacon and making oatmeal. Megan's job was to gather eggs in the hen house and then I would get them ready for scrambling. Megan hated that job because the chickens did not like her taking their eggs and would fly at her when she took them from the nest.

After breakfast we would hitch Dan up to the wagon that the Beecher's called the carryall. It would fill up with books and papers and lunches and children and big people and make its way to the Western Female Institute in the city. And then the day really began with lessons in geometry and literature and chemistry and history and language. I loved this part and the day seemed to fly by. Megan was still studying reading in McGuffy's reader. She was beginning to do well and her writing was improving.

After school I would go to Dr. Drake's if he was in town. I was learning more and more there and I think he was beginning to depend on me for many things. Megan would go with the other children in the carryall back to Walnut Hills where there would be chores waiting for her to do in the kitchen. And besides all this, Euleen and I continued to help in the Underground Railroad whenever we were needed.

As winter approached, our little room attached to the barn grew colder and colder. If it was very cold, the water in our wash basin and in Dan's pail froze. Megan and I discovered that if we got dressed standing up close to Dan and Bossie their bodies warmed us a bit and made dressing easier. The worst was running in the cold to the outhouse to do what we had to do.

"I don't even like that now," said Johnnie "but I hear that some people are getting indoor plumbing in their houses. I sure would like that."

"Wouldn't we all like that," I said. "Maybe someday we will have it too."

"What about Christmas? Tell us about Christmas," said Andrew. "Did you have a Christmas?"

"Of course we had a Christmas. We always had Christmas but that year it was a very special one, one that I will never forget."

9
CHRISTMAS REUNION

*T*HE Christmas season was drawing near. I had been able to save just a little bit from the money that I earned at Dr. Drake's but not nearly enough for all the presents that I wanted to buy. I wanted to get Miss Harriet a few pens because she was forever losing hers and her writing was so important for money for the family. I wanted to buy Megan a winter coat. She was outgrowing the one she had; her sleeves just barely covered her elbows and the bottom of the coat stopped just above her knees. It was getting so thin that she always shivered with cold. Sometimes the girls at school made fun of her. If I had enough money, I would fill both pockets with sweets. Megan loved all things sweet but they were a rare treat for us. And for Euleen, I would get her a brand new dress. I had never seen her in a new dress. She was always wearing clothes that other people threw away. I wanted to give her a dress of her very own. But all that was just dreaming. I didn't have nearly enough money.

Until one day on my way to Dr. Drake's office I passed a store called Japps that sold wigs and brushes. A small sign in the corner of the window said:

WILL PAY GOOD MONEY FOR HAIR
INQUIRE WITHIN

My hair was still 'flyaway" but it was long and thick. I hesitated to go in, afraid that they would tell me they had no use for my hair. I will never know if I don't ask, I thought.

The woman behind the counter took one look at me and said, "Oh dear, oh my."

I turned to leave, I didn't want to hear her next words asking me why I thought someone would want to buy my hair.

"Don't go," she said quickly. "Are you willing to sell your hair?"

"I would consider it," I answered

"We have a customer, an older woman who is looking for hair just your shade. She needs a wig badly. I can pay you good money."

"What is good money?" I asked.

"Five dollars?"

I could not believe it when I heard myself say, "I am afraid that is not enough."

"Would you sell it for ten dollars?" she said.

Ten dollars! I could buy all the presents for everyone and have money left over.

Calmly, I said, "Yes, I think that will work. However, you must give me the money first and a bonnet to cover my hair after you cut it."

"Sit right down then," she said as she handed me a ten dollar bill. She rummaged behind the counter for a pair of scissors. She found them and quickly started cutting huge clumps of hair from my head without any kind of design in mind, a clump here and a clump there.

When she announced that she had enough, I looked in the mirror and thought I was going to cry, but then, for some reason, it all seemed so funny, hilarious. I laughed instead. I looked like Dan did after those nasty people clipped his mane. My hair would grow back just like his did. I had money for presents and an old lady somewhere had a new wig. I took my ten dollars, put on my bonnet and left the store smiling. When I got to Dr. Drake's he wondered why I was keeping my hat on and I said, "Awfully cold today, keeps me warm."

That afternoon while I was at Dr. Drake's, Euleen came around to tell me that Mr. Birney said there would be a "parcel" arriving on Christmas night. It could be a big one and we might have to ask the Beechers if we could use the carryall.

I was sure that the Beechers would be agreeable and I told Euleen I would pick up her up at 8:00 Christmas night .

Christmas day dawned in Walnut Hills with gentle light and just a whisper of snow. I put Megan's present at the foot of our bed so she would see it when she woke up. She rolled over, rubbed away the sleep from her eyes, saw the box and jumped out of bed.

"Is it for me?"

"It has your name on it, doesn't it?"

"Yes, but may I open it now?"

"Right now."

She tore away the ribbons and pretty wrapping paper

and slowly opened the box.

"Oh, Littsie, look, it is a new coat, a beautiful new coat. May I put it on?"

"That is what coats are for."

Megan slipped into the coat. It was truly a lovely coat, navy blue with red velvet on the sleeves and collar and shiny brass buttons marching down the front. It fit her perfectly.

When she put her hands in the pockets she found the sweets I had put there.

"Sweets," she exclaimed. "Oh lovely, lovely sweets. Oh, perfect. And the coat is so warm. I am never going to take it off. However did you get it?"

"I will tell you someday," I said, as I adjusted my nightcap.

"May I wear it now?"

"Not to gather the eggs and help clean the stall, silly, you must wear your old coat for that. But you may wear it when we go to the Beecher's for Christmas breakfast."

Megan jumped up and said, "Littsie, you are the best sister ever a girl could have. As she gave me a big hug around the neck, my night cap came tumbling off and lay alone on the floor."

Megan screamed, "Littsie, where is your beautiful hair?"

"By now it is probably happily on the head of an old lady."

"How did it get on an old lady's head?"

"I sold my hair to a wig maker."

"Whatever for?"

"Money, money for Christmas presents."

"Littsie," she said. "You are the best, the very best. But I don't have anything for you," she said, looking up at me, upset and embarrassed. As she stood among the paper and ribbons in her new coat, she said, "I have an idea. I could wind the ribbons in what is left of your hair. I think I could make it look pretty good so that most people would not notice how short it is. Could that be my Christmas present to you?"

"If you think you can," I said. "Go ahead and try, presents come in many forms."

And Megan wound the red and green ribbons carefully through my hair. Even as a little girl she could work wonders with her hands. It really did hide the shortness of it. Actually, it looked very festive.

"Merry Christmas, Littsie," she said.

"Merry Christmas, Megan," I said.

"And Merry Christmas, Dan."

"Merry Christmas, Bossie."

"Merry Christmas, cat."

"Merry Christmas, chickens."

"Merry Christmas, owls."

"Merry Christmas, swallows," we called at the top of our voices.

Morning chores do not stop just because it is Christmas. We still had to feed Dan and Bossie, clean the stalls and gather eggs. The whisper of snow began to increase and as we did our chores, it softly covered the roof of the barn, gathered in the corner of windows and swirled around the chimney of the house. When we finished up, while the many bells of Cincinnati rang out with Christmas joy, we crossed the snow covered yard to the house, Megan in her new coat and I in my ribbons.

As we entered the house ready to help with breakfast, we were surrounded by the smells of a Christmas kitchen: roasting turkey, sage and onion, mince pies, apple pies, cranberries, chestnut stuffing, cookies and cinnamon. We peeked through the kitchen door and could see the dining room table set with the best china and an evergreen centerpiece dancing down the middle. Candles were everywhere. And in the parlor a great fire roared in the fireplace and dinner plates sat nearby for warming. Mysteriously the doors to Reverend

Beecher's study were closed. I had never seen them closed before. His study was always open to everyone.

The house was full of family and friends: Uncle Sam Foote, Aunt Elizabeth, Aunt Esther, Mary Dutton, Reverend Beecher and his wife, Henry Beecher, Miss Catherine, Charles Beecher and the little Beechers: Isabelle, Thomas and James and of course, Mr. Calvin Stowe. Miss Harriet saw us and came running with Christmas hugs.

"Merry Christmas, O'Donnell girls, and don't you look like Christmas itself with your hair all in ribbons, Littsie? Your hair looks lovely."

"Thank you," I said with a smile and a nudge to Megan. "Miss Harriet," I said, "I have a small gift for you," and I handed her my package.

"Thank you so much," she said. When she opened it and found the pens inside she was delighted. "Do you know how often I need these?" she asked.

"Yes, Ma'am, I've watched you when you are writing. Your writing is so important. I thought you could use them. Merry Christmas."

She smiled and gave me another Christmas hug.

After we all sat down and had a special Christmas breakfast with pancakes and bacon and eggs and sausages, Uncle Sam Foote announced that it was time for the Christmas parade.

"Whatever could that be?" I asked Megan as they all followed Uncle Sam's instructions.

Led by Reverend Beecher with his fiddle there

followed little James Beecher with a tin trumpet, Aunt Elizabeth with a clarinet, Miss Harriet with a tin kettle, Thomas with a bass drum, Aunty Esther with a rattle, Miss Catherine with a whistle, Miss Dutton with spoon and pan, Mr. Stowe with bells, Isabelle with tambourine, Mina with pot covers and Henry with a bugle.

"You join too," they said and handed us several spoons to bang together.

Megan and I joined in, at first a bit shy but we quickly got in the spirit of it all and banged our spoons together following the parade around the kitchen, through the dining room, on into the parlor, out to the snow covered front porch and back again. What noise we made as we played our "instruments" and giggled at the idea of it all. We sang *Good King Wenceslas* and *God Rest Ye Merry Gentlemen* and whatever else came to mind. When it was all over Uncle Samuel wished everyone "good fires and plenty of apples and nuts, not to mention mince pies and roast turkeys, long lives and merry evenings."

"And now," announced the Reverend Beecher, "is the time."

"The time for what?" they all called.

"The time to open my study doors. I want everyone, and I mean everyone, not just the children, to close their eyes. Are you ready? James, you are peeking. We can't open the doors until everyone has their eyes closed. Ready?"

"Now you may look."

I opened my eyes and there in the study, right in the center of the room was a most beautiful Christmas tree. I had never seen a Christmas tree. It stood there, waiting to be admired, with its top climbing right to the ceiling and its branches loaded with paper ornaments and popcorn and cranberries. It was hung all over with candy and small cakes, toys, nuts, pen wipes, small books, dolls and toy drums and an envelope for each of us. I thought I saw the tree take a bow.

And then the Reverend Beecher distributed all the gifts. In my envelope was a silver dollar and there was one for Megan too. And we received cakes and nuts and pen wipes. What fun everyone had opening gifts! It was lovely all together.

As things became a bit quieter, I took Miss Harriet aside and asked if Euleen and I could use the carryall that night as we had "work" for Mr. Birney and it could be large.

"It has been snowing so much and is getting

deeper, Littsie, why don't you take the sleigh that Mr. Perkins has loaned us? The snow will be just right and I think it will be easier on Dan."

"Thank you, Miss Harriet," I said with a smile. "It sounds like a good idea. I have always wanted to ride in a sleigh. What a better time than Christmas."

The rest of the morning and early afternoon Megan and I helped in the kitchen preparing the Christmas dinner. What a menu it was: roast turkey, cranberries, mashed potatoes, biscuits, green beans, applesauce, cherry pie, mince pie and Christmas cake. It was all delicious.

I think it was the best Christmas I had ever had.

"Was it better than the ones we have?" asked Andrew.

"Oh, no," I said. "How could it be better? We have you now and that makes all the difference."

Andrew smiled and moved in a little closer to me.

After the Christmas dinner dishes were washed and the kitchen cleaned, I quietly left the house and headed for the barn to get Dan hitched to the sleigh. It was good that he was such a fine work horse, so calm and willing. We asked him to do a lot. The air was turning colder so I put a horse blanket on him and I checked to see if there was one in the sleigh. To my delight, I found that Mr. Perkins had provided a warm buffalo blanket and way in the back seat was a small Christmas tree. That will help, I thought. It will look like we are just celebrating Christmas instead of rescuing enslaved people. I tucked Euleen's present under the blanket and grabbed my scarf, hat and mittens.

Just as I was about ready to leave, Mina came into the barn. "I was able to get some of the leftovers for you," she said quietly. "You might get hungry. And also I have heated this brick by the fire, it will keep your feet warm in the sleigh."

I looked carefully at her. Did she know what I was doing? Did she know about the Underground Railroad? I wasn't sure but I knew that whoever we were going to find that night might be hungry.

"Thanks," I said, "thanks a lot."

Mina smiled and went on back to the house.

As I guided Dan from the house and out onto the road, the snow had turned to flurries and stars were twinkling through the black velvet sky. Silent clouds skidded in view and whispering snowflakes climbed over my face and into my ribboned hair. The forest where we had played in the summer was dressed in brilliant snow that reflected the light of the moon. It was holiday peaceful and as Dan trotted along, I thought of all the people that had helped Megan and me and I was grateful, grateful for Christmas and friends and sisters and books and ribbons and horses and school and snowy nights.

Dan stopped as we came to the ridge overlooking the city as if he wanted to look at the view. At the bottom of the hill lay Cincinnati covered with a blanket of snow. The full moon lit the many church steeples, the houses with smoke curling from their chimneys, and the river beyond. The city shimmered in the snowy moon light.

"Beautiful, isn't it, Dan?" I said, " But you know we have a lot of work to do tonight, giddyup, now."

Good old Dan did as I asked and trotted on into the city. As we made our way to the Longworth house to pick up Euleen, you could certainly tell that it was Christmas in Cincinnati. There were candles in every window and wreaths on every door. Folks were gathered in various spots singing Christmas carols and when we passed by the well lit houses we could see people inside with family and friends enjoying this Christmas night.

Dan took us to the back of the Longworth house and I quickly got out and knocked on the kitchen door. Euleen answered almost immediately with her hands wrapped around a large bundle.

"Cook says I can have these leftovers," she said. "I think she may know what we are up to. She is a friend of Mr. Casey. Isn't it interesting how many people help in a quiet way with the Underground Railroad?" she asked.

"Yes," I said, "Mina has given us a parcel too. At least tonight the folks we help will eat well. Are you ready to go?"

"I am," she said as she put on her coat and scarf and followed me outside.

"Spandy! Littsie, you have a sleigh. How did that happen?"

"Mr. Perkins lent it to Miss Harriet. She said I could use it. It just slides right along. The snow is perfect for it and it makes it easier for Dan."

"And it is fun as well," said Euleen as Dan trotted his way back to the street. "Where do we go first?"

"We have to stop by Mr. Birney's house. He will tell us exactly."

Mr. Birney's home was not far away. When we got there we could hear singing and we could see people dancing and laughing around the fireplace in the parlor. Euleen knocked softly and in just a few minutes Mr. Birney came to the door.

"Merry Christmas, girls," he said. "I hope you have been enjoying this jolly day. Are you warm enough? This journey may be a little longer than usual. We hope that four people will be able to cross the river tonight. It is frozen pretty solid and that helps. You are to meet them on the riverbank about two miles from town. Take them on to the Columbia Road. Are you familiar with that road?"

"Yes, Sir," I said, "I have taken it many times."

"There is a small house nearby that has an eagle on the weathervane on top of the barn. The folks there said they could help and lead our "parcel" to the next station. There will be a lantern in the window. The pass word is still *The Boatman Dance*."

"Is there anything else we should know?"

"Yes, these slaves have been traveling for a good bit and will probably be cold and hungry. Here take my coat and my gloves, they may need them. I am glad that you have the sleigh. It will move through the snow a little faster, just in case they are being chased by slave catchers." Reaching into his pocket, he said, "They will need at least a little money, give them this."

"Thanks, Mr. Birney," I said, "we will do our best."

"You girls have done grand work for the Underground Railroad and the best part is no one suspects you," he said, as he tucked the buffalo blanket around us. "You'd better get going now, the snow has started again and the wind has picked up. Go on ahead, Dan."

Dan lifted his head and with a gentle pull we started for the river. The moon was bright enough to light the way but the snow, coming down so heavily and quickly, made it difficult to see. The reins were getting stiff and difficult to move. I trusted Dan to find the right way.

As we approached the river's edge, I looked for a place that we could hide until we saw the "parcel" crossing the river. Near the riverbank, I saw an old barn half falling down. It could hide us and also give a bit of shelter. I got off the sleigh and pulled Dan into the small area that was still standing. He was happy to be out of the snow and shook his head in approval. Euleen and I shared the buffalo blanket and kept an eye on the river. The wind was blowing hard now and whistling as it came around the corners of the barn. We could hear the ice on the river cracking and groaning as ice flows hit one another.

"I am glad I don't have to cross that river tonight," I said.

"I would cross anything, in any kind of weather, at any time of night, if it meant that I did not have to be a slave," said Euleen softly. "Nothing is as bad as being owned by someone else."

I could only imagine how that would be and I shivered to think of it.

We waited for quite a long time and when we were just ready to give up we saw a very tiny light in the middle of the river and just the outlines of people.

"Come on," said Euleen, "I think our parcel is here."

We ran in the dark right up to the river and whispered hellos from the shore to the shadows of people. They were crossing the ice with great care, as fast as they could, and looking over their shoulders to see if they were being followed. They had to be aware of everything around them. If they slipped off the ice and into the water there would be no way that we could help them and it wouldn't take long for the cold water to freeze their bodies. I kept thinking of the story of the lady with the baby that Reverend Rankin told us. Euleen and I tried to be very quiet so that we would not alarm or distract them. We just gave a low whistle so that they would know where we were.

When the group of people finally came to the shore we could see that it was a man and a woman and two children, a boy and a girl. But that was all we could make out. The man had his hat pulled low to keep out the cold and to hide his face. The woman and the children wore their scarves around their faces and huddled together.

"Follow us," we whispered.

"Do you have a password?" they asked.

"*The Boatman Dance*," we replied.

"Great God in the morning," the man said. "We made it. We made it to free soil, Celia." And he put his arm around his wife and children and said again, "We made it. We made it."

"Oh, Willis, we did indeed! We did indeed! We all made it safely and we made it together."

"But we must hurry," I said to them. "We need to get you to a safe house just in case there are slave catchers not far behind. Quickly now, follow us to the barn."

As we led the way through the snow and the wind, I noticed that Euleen was strangely quiet. Most times she would talk to those we helped, explaining all that would happen and telling them where they were and what to expect. But she was silent.

When we got to the barn I encouraged them to sit down and catch their breath for just a moment. As the man took off his hat I noticed Euleen's face change with astonishment but she remained quiet.

The woman said, "If only Letty were here, then the whole Randolph family would all be together."

Euleen slowly walked toward the woman and took off her scarf to reveal her face and said, "We are all together, Mama."

The woman looked closely at Euleen

"Is it you, Letty? Is it truly you? Oh Lord, child, I thought I would never see you again. I have cried for you since the day master took you away and sold you. Is it you or am I seeing things?"

"Yes, Mama, it is truly me," said Euleen. "Remember how you gave us a secret name in case we got taken away, a secret name that would identify us so you would know us if we ever found each other? When we met you at the river, I thought there was something familiar in Papa's voice and in the way you walked but I could not let myself believe it. When you said 'If only Letty were here' I knew. That was the secret name you gave me."

With that there was such jubilation and joy and while the wind howled around the barn the five of them kissed and cried and hugged and hugged some more. Euleen was introduced to the brother and sister she had never met because she was sold before they were born.

"What a Christmas present," she said, "a brother and a sister, Aaron and Betsey."

I was so happy for them all. I was so happy to be part of the Underground Railroad that reunited them and on Christmas at that. When Euleen's Papa began to sing with joy, I had to stop him. "Someone could hear you," I said and they might not be friendly.

It was Euleen who realized that we had to keep moving and she explained that to her family.

"Hold on, hold on one minute," her papa said. "Could I give one suggestion? You see that tree in the sleigh. If we tied that to the back of the sleigh, low enough to touch the ground, it would hide our tracks as we went along."

"Yes, yes," I said. "That is a great idea."

We found a piece of rope in the barn and Mr. Randolph tied the tree to the sleigh. It worked perfectly so that you could not see horse or sleigh tracks.

Then the whole group piled into the sleigh and we wrapped the buffalo blanket around everyone and headed out into the snow, the Christmas tree covering our tracks. I tell you that sleigh was full of so much joy I think it could have flown to the safe house.

As Euleen and her family talked and laughed, I guided Dan up to the Columbia Road. The snow was still coming down hard and Dan had to constantly shake his head so he could see where he was going. It continued to get colder and I wrapped my scarf tighter around my neck. I was so glad that Mina had given us the warmed brick.

Shortly we arrived at the house that Mr. Birney said would take our "parcel". The eagle on the weather vane sat atop the barn covered in snow so I knew it was the right house. But it was a bit worrisome because there was not a light anywhere and everything was too quiet for Christmas night. I told the others to stay warm in the sleigh and I got out to investigate. I walked up the steps and crossed the snow covered porch to the door and knocked, softly at first and then a little louder. There was no answer. I tried the door and it opened. I called out, "Anyone here?"

As I walked slowly across the room, I heard a man snoring and I turned to see a man asleep on the floor with a bottle in his hand. He turned over in his sleep and I froze with fear. It was that same nasty man, the man who had threatened me on the steamboat, the man who hurt Dan, the man that was in the crowd the night of the abolition meeting.

Be Thou between me and all things grisley,
Be Thou between me and all things mean
Be Thou between me and the gruesome,
Come with me.

I whispered as I rubbed Mama's ring. When I got my wits about me, I backed out of the house and slowly closed the door and ran to the sleigh.

"Giddyup, Dan, and run with all you have," I said.

Dan sensed the urgency and galloped through the

snow as fast as I had ever seen him go. Euleen's family became quiet and frightened and Euleen kept asking what was going on.

"It was that mean man," I yelled over the sound of the wind, "the one that beat Dan. There must have been a huge mistake. Mr. Birney would never have sent us to a man like that. Never."

"But now what do we do?" asked Euleen.

"I think I know just the place. We are half way there now and if Dan can make it the rest of the way and there are not too many snow drifts, it will work just fine."

"What are you talking about?" said Euleen, struggling to be heard above the wind.

"My mama's and papa's farm," I said. "We will go there. I doubt if slave catchers would think to go there."

When we had covered a pretty good distance I let Dan slow down. The snow was deeper and it was a struggle for him to pull his heavy load. His nostrils were white with frost and snow had gathered on his eyelashes and was beginning to ice his feet. But he kept going. There was never a better horse than Dan. That horse would do anything you asked.

And he did it. He got us to our little cabin at the farm. The whole lot of us tumbled out of the sleigh and trudged through the snow and almost fell through the front door. I was so glad to be home.

"Make yourselves comfortable," I said. "First, I must take care of Dan. He deserves it."

I took my good friend into the barn and unhitched him from the sleigh. He was glad to be rid of it and shook his body with delight. I was beginning to rub him down when I realized that because of all his hard work he was sweating. I knew that the combination of the extreme cold and his hot sweating body might make him sick. There was only one thing to do. Let him come into the house so he could be near the fire. It was the least I could do.

"You took a horse into the house?" squealed the children.

"Yep, right into the house. It was the only thing to do."

"But what about the poop?" asked Andrew.

"We cleaned it right up. It really was not much of a problem."

"Don't talk about poop," said Isabelle. "Go on with your story, Grandma."

By the time I got him in the cabin, Euleen's papa had started a fire. It filled the whole room with welcome warmth and light. Euleen was heating up some of the food that Mina had given us. Euleen's mother could not keep her eyes off Letty. She could hardly believe this was happening.

I pulled out some of Mama's best dishes and set the table. I even found a few candles. It almost looked as good as the Beecher's Christmas table.

Euleen's papa said, "I know just what we need," and put his coat on and went back outside. In just a few minutes he came back with the tree from the sleigh.

"A Christmas tree!" everyone yelled.
"A Christmas tree!"

"Let's use our hats and scarves and mittens for decoration," suggested Aaron. "It will make it festive." And it did just that. We wound our scarves round and round and stuck our hats and mittens on the branches. I found some paper and scissors and we made a few more decorations. Euleen's mama made a big star and put it right on the top.

"We followed the North Star to get here," she said, "and look where it stopped. Right on top of our Christmas tree. Who would have believed it?"

"Is that why you always put a paper star at the top of your tree, Grandma?" asked Anne.

"Yes, darling," I said. "I never want to forget that Christmas when a family found freedom and their daughter."

"Then what happened?" the rest of the children asked.

Oh, yes, I remembered Euleen's present and brought it in from the sleigh and put it under the Christmas tree.

When she opened it she couldn't stop smiling. "But Littsie" she said looking at me hard, how did you do this?" Then she noticed my hair. "You didn't," she said. "You didn't do it. You didn't sell your hair?"

"Yes," I said laughing and it has taken you all day to notice. "Didn't Megan do a good job hiding how short it is? It will grow back. Now go ahead and put your dress on."

She did and it fit her perfectly. She looked so nice and she wore it to our Christmas meal.

And that was some meal that Mina provided: turkey, potatoes, cranberries, biscuits, applesauce, pies and even some of the Christmas cake. The fire warmed us and the food filled us and Dan cheered us. There was a lot of talk at that meal. Euleen told her folks what had happened to her since that awful day when she was sold. She told them how we met when the steamboat that she was on with her master blew up, how I got her out of the water and eventually got her to Mr. Longworth who freed her. When they asked about me and my family I told them about the cholera epidemic and about losing and finding Megan and how we now lived with the Beechers and about working with Dr. Drake.

"Child," Mrs. Randolph said, "You have had a hard time, a hard time. I know one thing for sure, your mama and papa would be so proud to see all you have done and especially what you are doing tonight. They must have been good people, your mama and papa."

"Yes, they were," I said, "the best. But do you know why I am so happy tonight? I am so happy to see our house filled with a family again, just like it used to be."

When we were finished and, oh, so full of food, Mr. Randolph quietly asked when they would be leaving for the next "safe house."

"I have been giving that some thought," I said. "By all rights you should leave first thing in the morning. But I don't see why you couldn't live here in this house permanently. I don't think we were followed at all. Everyone around thinks this house is empty. It would be perfect. There is a bedroom for you and Mrs. Randolph and there is the loft for the children. It would help me out too, knowing someone was here."

"Well, Miss Littsie, you might have something there," Mr. Randolph said. "I don't think we were followed either. You see we left about ten days before Christmas when Master and his family left to spend Christmas in Richmond with their relatives. Master won't even miss us for a few more days. And one more thing, if you don't mind my saying it, I can see that your place needs some work. I was a carpenter on the plantation. I know a thing or two. I could be doing the fixin, around here."

"Do you know about crops and such too?" I asked.

"Yes Ma'am, I have worked in the fields planting all kinds of things."

"Do you think you could plant our fields in the spring?"

"Sure could."

"What if you kept 75% of the profit and I kept 25%?

Does that sound fair?"

"Yes, ma'am. It sounds fair to me. What do you think, Euleen?"

"I think it is the best deal I have ever heard," said Euleen. "It will be wonderful to know that my parents are close by."

"Then it is a deal," I said, as I shook hands with Mr. Randolph. I was relived to know that the place would be looked after. Megan would be able to visit more often and we would be getting a little bit of money. I slept that night up in the loft with Euleen and her brother and sister. As I lay looking at the moon through the window that Papa had so carefully placed for just such a view, I thought of all that had happened since the first time I slept there. I was only eleven then and now I was close to fifteen. I yawned and rolled over and thought, you are growing up, Littsie girl, yes you are.

Euleen and I left very early the next morning. We needed to get back before anyone missed us, before the Beechers or the Longworths woke up. Euleen's mama got up with us and gave us some food for the journey and I remembered to give Mr. Randolph the money Mr. Birney had given us for him.

"It is from Mr. Birney," I said. "He is another one of those good people."

"Please tell him thank you for me," said Mr. Randolph. "He will never know how much this means to the family."

Euleen's mama put her arms around her daughter

and said, "You come back now, girl, you hear? I don't ever want to lose you again."

" Mama, I'll be back, don't you worry," said Euleen giving her a big hug.

Dan had rested and was ready to go. We hitched him to the sleigh, said our goodbyes and started the journey back to Cincinnati. The snow had stopped during the night and now the sun shone with a frosty light. Dan took us quickly over a wonderland of drifts and icicles and snow blanketed meadows that stretched to where the soft rising hills stood covered in snow, like so many piles of sugar. Euleen and I sang *The Boatman Dance* at the top of our voices all the way home.

When we got back into the city, it was very quiet. Folks were still sleeping. I took Euleen to the Longworth's and then went to the Beecher's. I put Dan in his stall and then quietly slid into bed next to Megan and went fast asleep.

I tell you that was some Christmas.

10
A NEW FRIEND

*I*N January Miss Harriet Beecher married Mr. Calvin Stowe.

"So you were right, they definitely were "sweet on each other," said Isabelle. "Was it a big wedding, Grandma?"

"No, it was very small. Only her family and Miss Dutton were there. It was a great surprise to us all. Now her name would be Mrs. Harriet Beecher Stowe."

"Hmmm, that name sounds so familiar," said Johnnie. "Oh yes, we read her book, *Uncle Tom's Cabin*, in school. It was a good one and come to think of it, it had the same story that Reverend Rankin told you, the one about the lady and the baby on the ice."

"Yes," I said, "that is where she got the idea for *Uncle Tom's Cabin*. That book sold millions of copies all over the world. And do you know it is one of the things that helped end slavery? Isn't it amazing what just one person can do?"

"And you were right there when she was writing and getting ideas," said Anne.

"Yes, I was, yes indeed I was."

"It is getting awfully late now, children. I think you ought to get ready to go to bed," I said.

"Oh no, Grandma," they all said. "It is so hot and muggy, we won't be able to sleep anyway. Please, please go on with your story."

"Maybe just a bit more but first let me get a little more lemonade."

Let's see, I said as I came back to my rocker, that was the winter when I met Elizabeth Blackwell. She was a new girl in town and just my age. She and her family had come from England. I liked her the minute I met her. It was amazing how many of the same interests we had. Her father had been involved with sugar plantations but when he saw how terrible the slaves on the sugar plantations were treated he came to the United States. He wanted to set up a place to make sugar in a free state, one that didn't have slavery. That is why he brought his family to Cincinnati. The Blackwell family wanted to end slavery and so did I.

And don't you know, Elizabeth was very interested in medicine too. Sometimes I would take her with me to Dr. Drake's and show her all that I had learned. She was eager to know everything.

She was not in Cincinnati very long. Her father died shortly after they got here and they had to move. But do you know what? She became the first woman ever to graduate from medical school in the United States. She had to apply to 30 schools before one would take her. You see women were not permitted to go to medical school. The one that did take her did so as a joke. The joke was on them though, she graduated first in her class. And I was there to see her graduate. I tell you I was so proud of her.

"Now, off to bed with the lot of you. I will tell more tomorrow night, I promise."

The following night, I thought the children would forget my promise because they were so busy catching fireflies. The little bugs illuminated the dark with a small but joyful light. It always made me smile to watch them.

In a bit the children grew tired of their hunt and flopped in the chairs on the porch.

"You have to keep your promise, Grandma," they said. "Continue with your story."

"Yes," I said, "I know, I promised and I don't make promises unless I can keep them. Where was I?"

"Miss Harriet had gotten married and you met Elizabeth Blackwell," they answered.

Oh, yes, the winter. Well, all during that winter Euleen and I made many visits to her family and Megan often came with us. They were doing just fine. Mr. Randolph had done a lot of "fixin" and the O'Donnell place was looking good. As spring approached, I asked Mr. Randolph if he would like to borrow Dan to plow the fields and keep them ready to be seeded.

"That would be just fine," he said. "I have watched your Dan and I know he will be good with the plow." So one day in April I rode Dan out to the farm. He was happy to be there and to be doing something a little different. But knowing that the Beecher's would need him, I told Mr. Randolph that I would have to take him back in about three weeks.

"That will be plenty of time for me to get the

plowing done," Mr. Randolph said. "And remember, Miss Littsie, you will get 25% of the profit that the crops bring in, just like we agreed."

I was glad that he remembered the deal we had made. Dr. Drake had been making several trips out of town and when he did, it meant that I did not make as much money. Megan was growing and growing and needed clothes and shoes. We were grateful that we could stay at the Beecher's. It helped a great deal but they did not have extra money to give away. Megan and I were doing without new clothes and shoes and lots of other things that children need.

"Were you poor, Grandma?" asked one of the children.

"Yes, dear, we were very poor. I was awfully anxious for the crop at the farm to come in. But that was going to be a long wait."

One day, it must have been late spring, Megan came running into our room in the barn all excited.

"Littsie, oh Littsie, guess what?"

"Tell, tell," I said.

"I got a job at the cotton mill. You know, the one near the canal. I will be helping to spin the cotton into yarn."

" Megan, now be serious. They don't take children as young as you."

"Yes, yes they do. They even told me that they like to hire children because we can do things and get to places that big people can't. Just think, we will have some extra money."

"I don't know about this, Megan," I said. "Will you still be able to help the Beechers and also go to school?"

"Yes, yes," she said jumping up and down with excitement. "They said I could work after school until summer and then I can work all day."

I was hesitant to give my approval but then I remembered that Megan was now almost nine and I had seen many children her age working. I was not much older when I was working for Dr. Gilbert.

"Alright," I said, "but it can't interfere with your school work. Do you understand?"

" Littsie," she said, throwing her arms around me. "You will see. I will make lots of money and maybe next Christmas it will be your turn to have a new coat."

And so that spring Megan started working in the cotton mill.

11
A SERIOUS BUSINESS

THAT spring and summer Euleen and I continued to help Mr. Birney whenever he needed us. I remember one July night very clearly. It was hot and muggy and the air was very still, not a breeze anywhere. A small fog had formed near the river and rolled up the banks and into the streets. Euleen, Dan and I were coming back from taking escaped slaves to the Dumas House when, through the misty fog, we could make out a large crowd gathered at Mr. Birney's office. Their angry faces were lit by the torches they carried. They were yelling and shaking their fists. Euleen and I were very frightened. This was the kind of thing that we knew could turn violent. The crowd would definitely see us if we tried to go around them so we quickly hid with Dan between two buildings and watched.

"You can just get out of town, Birney," they were shouting. "You are nothing but a trouble maker and a darky lover," they shouted.

"Your paper is full of lies and falsehoods. Did the devil teach you how to write? You should be tarred and feathered."

"We don't need your kind in Cincinnati. Go on, get out," a familiar voice called. I looked at all the faces in the crowd and saw that same nasty man, the one that I kept running into. The torch he was carrying lit his face clearly. He was dark haired with a scraggily beard, tiny mean looking eyes, a full red face that looked cruel and cunning. He was leading the crowd and urging them on. Suddenly some men burst through the door and got into the office. They tore up all Mr. Birney's papers, broke the windows and threw printer's type out on the street. Before I knew it they had taken the printing press and pulled it apart. They took the pieces and marched down to the river and threw them right into the water.

"That good for nothing abolitionist won't be able to write against slavery any more," they shouted and laughed.

"Just let him try, we'll show that confounded darky lover."

"Do you think Mr. Birney is in there?" Euleen whispered.

"I don't think so," I replied as I rubbed my ring.

After a bit the crowd grew tired and broke up and started wandering away. Just when we thought it was all over and all the people had gone, we saw the nasty man go back into the building. He was not there long but when he came out he was carrying Mr. Birney's cash box. He stopped as he came out of the door and stood on the steps and looked around. That is when he saw us. He snarled and came running toward us.

"You are that feisty girl I have been seeing everywhere," he hissed. "You little brat. Just like you to have a darky friend," he said as he gave Euleen a push. "You will see. Tonight we are going to burn some of those darkies' houses."

Dan was getting upset. He pushed himself between

the man and Euleen and me. When the man moved, we moved, keeping Dan between us. Suddenly Dan recognized the man as the one from the circus who had beaten him. He began to whiney and rear up.

"Control that animal," yelled the man. "Control him now, I say."

With that, Dan stood on his hind feet and came right down with all his weight on that awful man, snorting and whinnying. It was a scary sight. The man fell to the ground still holding onto Mr. Birney's cash box.

With all this commotion, people who lived in the

area came out of their houses to see what was going on. I held Dan's reins tight and tried to calm him down.

"What are you girls doing?" someone demanded.

"Do you see that man right there?" I said, pointing to the man on the ground. "We saw him steal Mr. Birney's cash box. See it is still with him. He tried to attack us when he saw us. My horse, Dan, protected us. Please get the police right now," I pleaded.

Someone ran to the nearby police station and brought back a policeman. By this time the man was beginning to stir and moan. When the policeman arrived he took one look and said, "Why, that is Jim Henry. He is part of that gang that has been attacking folks on flatboats coming down the river. He is a nasty one, that one. On Christmas night he robbed and ran folks right out of their house on the Columbia Road. We have been looking for him for a long while. Who is responsible for this?" he said, looking at the crowd.

"We are," I said softly. "We saw him urge the crowd to damage Mr. Birney's office and then we saw him come back and get the cash box that is still right there on the ground. He saw us and came after us but Dan here protected us."

Dan was still upset and kept shaking his head and snorting.

"Lucky you to have a horse like Dan. You did a good job but you should be more careful," the policeman said. "You two girls should not be out on the street this late. I want you to go on home now. I will take care of this scoundrel."

"Yes, Sir," we said, and turned to go. Just then Mr. Birney appeared. Someone had told him about the crowd and he had come to see for himself. He saw us and came running.

"Euleen, Littsie, are you alright?" he asked with great concern.

" Yes, Sir, yes, Sir. We are a little shaky but we are fine thanks to Dan. And we didn't let that man get your cash box. See it is still lying right there on the ground.

And we found out that he robbed those folks at the safe house on Christmas night. Ran them off, no wonder the house was empty except for him."

"Oh, my goodness," he said, "you girls are heroes, real true heroes. What would I do without you? Come now, come on into the office with me."

And then he saw his office, the windows broken, the door bashed in and pieces of press all over the street. He stooped and picked up some of the type and quietly shook his head. "What makes people do things like this?" he asked. "What makes them think this is alright? For that matter what makes them think slavery is alright? What makes them think it is their right to own another person? What if they themselves were owned by another person? This will not stop me. I will go on. I will keep writing against slavery. I cannot let this stop me."

Euleen walked up to him and said, "Thank you, Sir. Don't ever, ever stop."

Mr. Birney stooped down and put his hand on her shoulder and said, "I promise you, Euleen, by all that is holy, that I will never stop."

We rode Dan home that night almost without saying a word to each other. Euleen and I knew we were involved in some very serious business but we both knew that it was right and that we could depend on one another. We did not need to say it. Our silence and a hug said it all.

12
THE MILL

MEGAN worked a full day, six days a week that summer and she worked long hours. She would leave to go to the mill at 7:00 in the morning and she would not come back until 7:00 at night. She would be so tired she couldn't even eat. All she wanted to do was to go to bed. Sometimes she cried in her sleep.

"Megan," I said, one day, "tell me what you do at the cotton mill."

"They call me a scavenger. I have to get under the machinery and pick up any loose cotton, sweep, dust and clean oil spills." Proudly, she said, "Only children can be scavengers. Big people can't fit under the machine. I have to be very careful though because if you get to close to the machine, you can get hurt."

"How do you get hurt?"

"Once I saw a girl my age get her finger caught in the machine. It cut it right off and sometimes girls with long hair get it caught too. If you are not careful the machine will pull your hair out and even some of your scalp. That is why I wear my nightcap at work."

"I am not sure this is good for you," I said, bending down to look at her face. "You are always tired."

"I am fine," she said. "The only part I don't like is that we are not allowed to talk to each other and we never get a chance to rest. But guess who started working with us?"

"I am sure it wasn't Reverend Beecher."

"No, silly, it is Tommy O'Brien."

"Tommy is working at the mill?" I asked with surprise. "I wonder why. But I feel better knowing he is there. I am sure he will look out for you. I suppose you can continue, Megan, but it worries me."

"Don't worry, Littsie," she said. "I will be alright."

As summer continued she was not alright. The lack of fresh air and sunshine made her very pale. Sometimes I heard her softly crying in her sleep and, worst of all she was having a hard time breathing. I had learned at Dr. Drakes what to listen for in the chest and one night as she slept I put my ear close to her heart and could hear her wheezing. I have to find out what is going on at the mill, I thought.

The next day I found Tommy at the market juggling for the crowd. When he had a break I called to him.

"Tommy, Tommy, you still juggle? You are a busy man. Megan tells me you are working at the cotton mill too."

"That I am, Littsie, but not for much longer. I can't stand the place."

"Tell me what goes on there," I said. "I am worried about Megan."

"It is terrible, Littsie," he said. "It is always hot and dirty and the noise and clatter of the machines makes me crazy. And that overseer is a mean one. He won't let us talk to each other or take a short break. We are standing all the day. And if we break any of the rules he gets out his leather strap and beats us. And do you know, when some of the little children get drowsy and sleepy, he just takes those little ones and holds their heads in a big tub of water so that they wake up. He scares them so. One day, when one of the little boys tried to run away, he chained him to the machine."

I could hardly believe what I was hearing. How could anyone treat children that way?

"What is your job?" I asked.

"I am a piecer. When a thread breaks I lean over the machine and repair the broken threads. Even though I am pretty strong, it is hard to do. The machine is still running and if I am not careful I might loose a finger. And with all this nastiness, children are only paid half of what the adults are paid and we do the same thing."

"Megan is having trouble breathing," I said.

"Ah, she must have the 'mill fever'. Many of the children have it. It comes from breathing in all that cotton dust, gets in your lungs. I have heard some people call it brown lung. Littsie, you should get her out of the mill and soon. I am leaving next week."

I knew Tommy was right. I had to find a way. She couldn't work there anymore. We would have to find another way to make money.

That night when Megan came home and fell into bed exhausted and breathing hard, I told her she could not go back.

"But Littsie, what will we do? We won't have enough money. And you won't get a Christmas coat."

"Forget the coat," I said. "I can wear my old one. We will find a way," I said, as I held up Mama's ring. Putting my arms around her frail little body, I said, "You don't have to worry anymore. That overseer is not going to hurt you. It is all over and you are safe now. You never have to go back there again."

Megan fell into a deep sleep that night. She never cried in her sleep again. But each time I passed the mill and saw children going to work my heart ached.

13
HARD GOODBYES

*T*HE following week I said to Megan, "I know what would make you feel better. How about a day at the farm?"

"Yes, yes," said Megan, "I would love that but do you think it would be okay with Mrs. Stowe?"

"I don't think she will mind," I said.

I checked with Mrs. Stowe and she said it would be just fine. "Go on now and enjoy yourselves," she said.

We saddled up Dan, got Euleen and followed the road out to Columbia. It was a cool clear morning and the Ohio River curved like a blue ribbon between the hillsides. It was almost the end of summer and fresh, gentle breezes surrounded us. It was harvest time and farmers were bringing in corn, tomatoes, cucumbers, beans, hay and oats. As we came close to the farm we could see Mr. Randolph working in the fields. The harvest was good and plentiful.

When he saw us he stopped what he was doing and came to greet us. The whole family gathered round and said we must share lunch that came with this great harvest. They all looked so healthy, so much better than when we found them at Christmas. But I detected that something was worrying them; they were quieter than usual.

Once we had finished Mrs. Randolph's tasty lunch, I asked, "Is there something wrong? Is there something that we need to talk about?"

"I am afraid there is," Mr. Randolph said. "Last week when I went to the Columbia market I found this." He pulled a wrinkled piece of paper from his pocket and laid it on the table. "I can't read it well. We were not allowed to learn to read on the plantation. I do know that this word is my name, Willis, and that word is my wife, Celia."

$200 Dollar Reward Absconded from the service of Mr. Walker on, December 15th, 4 Negros answering to the following descriptions; **WILLIS**, a mildly dark negro man, age about 36 years, 5 feet 10 inches high, very strong with a pleasing face, a smart and active fellow. He has a scar on the right side of the face. He is a fine carpenter and also a good field hand. He was wearing blue broadcloth pants and a green jacket. **CELIA**, his wife, very strong made, an excellent seamstress, medium brown, age about 35 years, their son **AARON** about 8 years and their daughter, **BETSEY**. Any person or persons that will secure any information about the above mentioned slaves or manage to capture them shall have an immediate reward of $200. JAMES WALKER.

Euleen snapped the paper up and began to read.

For a moment we all stood in stunned silence. How could this be happening? Everything was going so well. The Randolphs had found their daughter, they had a home, the harvest was good and now this.

Mrs. Randolph cried out loud, "Willis, what are we going to do? I won't go back, never. What are we going to do?"

The children ran to her and held on to her skirts.

"It is worse than I thought," said Mr.

Randolph, "and now the folks around here know me. They know I have a scar on my face and I am sure they have seen me wear that green jacket. There will certainly be one who wants $200 more than my friendship."

"You are NOT going back there," said Euleen. "We know what to do, Littsie and I. We will get you to Canada no matter what. They can't get you there."

"Girl, you are being crazy," said her father. "How do you think we will get there? We have no horse or wagon and almost no money?"

"Some folks have walked there," said Euleen. "It is hard and long but they have made it."

"Oh, Lord," said, Mrs. Randolph. "Oh Lord, help us," she cried.

"Mr. Randolph," I said, "there is a wagon in the barn. I want you to take it, and," I said slowly and with some difficulty, "I want you to take Dan. He is big and strong. He can get you there and when you get your farm in Canada he can be your plow horse."

"But Littsie," said Euleen, "Dan is your best friend."

"I know," I said, "but so are you. This is the right thing. I know it. Please don't try to change my mind."

Mr. Randolph rose from the table and took my hand, "Miss Littsie, how can I ever thank you?"

"The only thanks I want is to know that you are safe. We don't have any time to lose. You must be ready to go by nightfall. The Underground Railroad always moves under the cover of darkness. You must take the road north to Springboro. There is a safe house there.

They will give you directions to the next safe house. But you must hurry to get ready. Who knows how many people have seen that ad?"

"I am going with you," said Euleen.

"Now girl, you better think about that," said her papa. "You are a free black girl and you are going to school and you have a job with Mr. Longworth."

"Papa, I have been away from my family for so long and now that I have found you, I never want to let you go."

Megan came and stood next to me and slipped her hand in mine. We knew what it meant to be separated from your family, we knew what Euleen meant.

"But you have it nice here," said her papa.

"I will have it nice in Canada too," she said. "Robert Duncanson said there are good schools there for Aaron and Betsey."

"Who is Robert Duncanson?" asked Mr. Randolph.

"A painter that I met," said Euleen.

Mr. Randolph scratched his head and said, "Euleen, you are one determined girl. I know you are right, we must go and quickly."

We spent the rest of the day packing the wagon with all that they would need. We covered their belongings with the harvest. They could sell it along the way and that would give them some money to get started. While we packed, Betsey kept a look out for anyone that might look like a slave catcher.

At dusk, as the last bits were being stuffed in, I said, "When you get to Canada look for the Wilberforce

Settlement. A group of Quakers from Cincinnati started that settlement for slaves that were escaping. They are good folk and will give you all the help you need."

Mr. Randolph turned to me and said, "Miss Littsie, we made a deal at Christmas time. I have left one fourth of the harvest in the barn for you. Now don't argue with me. It is yours fair and square. You have been more than kind to us and I keep my bargains. And one more thing, if by some way Dan is the father of a little horse, I will see that you get it, somehow."

They all climbed into the wagon and I gave Dan a big hug. I whispered thanks for all he had done for us and said that someday we would see each other again. Right now he had a special job to do. He seemed to understand and nuzzled my face. I thought my heart was going to jump out of my chest.

Euleen jumped down from the wagon for a last goodbye. "We have been through a lot," she said. "You better write me and tell me everything. And could you explain to Mr. Longworth? I will write him when we get to Canada." We gave each other hugs and she got in the wagon again.

"I never say goodbye," I said, "just take care."

The sun was going down in the western sky. Clouds of red and gold hung near the sun and washed across the horizon. Dan pulled the wagon off into the sunset and Megan and I waved until we couldn't see them anymore.

14
GROWN UP

"*T*HEN what?" asked the children.

"I was able to get a bit of money from the harvest that Mr. Randolph left and that meant that Megan and I could spend the rest of the summer at the farm. Megan's health improved a great deal; her cheeks got nice and rosy and her breathing improved.

Some of our old neighbors stopped by and when they heard that I had worked with Dr. Drake they came round asking for medical advice."

"Why didn't you go to medical school?" asked Johnnie.

"Because the schools did not admit women," I said. "Remember how I told you what a hard time Elizabeth Blackwell had?"

"This is 1884 and it is still hard for women to become doctors," said Isabelle.

When summer was over, we both went back to the Beecher's but things were changing there too. Harriet Beecher Stowe had twin baby girls, Hattie and Eliza. They were so cute. But they were a lot of work and Mrs. Stowe and her sister Catherine felt that so many other things were going on in their lives they would have to close their school. The Western Female Institute students went to the Ryland School. Megan and I did not make the change. I was at the age when people thought you could start taking care of yourself. After talking with Dr. Drake, I decided to go back to live at the farm and work as a nurse in the village. I would do what I could for people but if it became too difficult, I would get Dr. Drake. There was a public school now in Columbia and Megan could go to school there. And it would be free.

"Who took care of the farm,?" asked Johnnie.

"I made deals with neighbors just like I did with Mr. Randolph. It helped a lot."

"Did you ever hear from the Randolphs?"

"Yes, they got to Canada safely and after a bit at the Wilberforce Settlement they were able to have their own farm. They planted orchards, raised cattle and sowed grain. Their families still live there today. And oh, the best part, one day, probably five years after they left, there was a knock at our cabin door. And who was standing there but Euleen herself. I was so glad to see her. We just danced and danced. And tied to the hitching post out front was the prettiest horse you have ever seen, just the image of Dan. He was the same beautiful chestnut color and had the same full mane and tail."

"Remember Papa's promise," Euleen asked. "This is Dan's son and Papa has sent him to you. I rode him all the way from Canada."

I tell you tears rolled down my cheeks. I got right up on that young horse and rode him around the pasture. He was just like his father, strong, smart and gentle. I was so happy to have him.

Euleen and I visited for a long time. She did meet up with Robert Duncanson for just a bit. She said he was doing some murals for Mr. Longworth now and was becoming famous.

Euleen told me that she had gone to school in Canada and was a teacher in one of the farm schools. Mr. and Mrs. Randolph were just fine and the farm was quite prosperous. It was so good to see her and to know that all was well.

"Did Euleen have to walk back to Canada?" asked Andrew.

"No," I said, "by that time there were trains that could get her quite close."

"Was there still slavery and the Underground Railroad?"

"Oh my, yes," I said. "Slavery did not end for good until after the Civil War a little over 20 years ago. But end it did, no slaves anymore, anywhere in the USA. I like to think that the work Euleen and I did helped that happen.

"And Megan? Did she stay in Cincinnati?"

"That sister of mine did just fine. She grew up and married the Captain of a steamboat. I don't see her as often as I would like but we do keep in touch through letter writing."

"What about Tommy O'Brien?" asked Anne.

"You mean Tommy the Juggler? He came to Columbia and helped his family on their farm and then one day, when I was about 21, he juggled his way right into my heart."

"You mean he was sweet on you?"

"Sure was," came the answer from the kitchen and Grandpa came out to the porch and put his arm around me. "Still am," he said, as he picked up some fruit and juggled it.

" I get it," said Andrew, "that is why your name is O'Brien and not O'Donnell."

"I will always be an O'Donnell," I said, "but Littsie O'Donnell O'Brien isn't bad either. We have had a good life, Tommy and I. He made our farm give us food and extra money as well. I have been able to be a nurse to the people in Columbia and we have four wonderful children and four super grandchildren."

I sat back in the rocker and looked at the children. In the distance I could hear the horn of a steamboat and the whistle of a train as they passed through Cincinnati. It was a beautiful evening and the sky was full of the pinks and oranges of sunset. I smiled as I rubbed Mama's ring. I knew that the children would start to make their own stories now and I want to hear them all, every one of them.

The End

Authors' Note

Many people often ask what is actual history and what is fiction in Littsie's story. Although Littsie and her family and Euleen and her family are fiction, they represent families that could have had the same kind of experiences during this period of our country's history.

Characters such as Dr. Drake, Stephen Foster, Nicholas and Susan Longworth, Theodore Weld, Angelina Grimke, Dr. Locke, Mr. Proctor, John Rankin, James Birney, William Casey, Jacob Strader, Elizabeth Blackwell are all real and are portrayed accurately. The Beechers, their family and friends are real as are their events and activities. The Beecher home still stands today in the Walnut Hills area of Cincinnati,

Theodore Weld and Angelina Grimke married and remained extremely active in the abolitionist movement. James Birney remained an abolitionist and even ran for president as the candidate for the Liberty Party. John Rankin and his family are believed to have helped over 2,000 slaves escape to freedom. William Casey, a free black abolitionist, continued to help many escaping slaves cross the Ohio. Elizabeth Blackwell became the first woman in America to receive a medical degree.

The artist Robert Duncanson lived and worked off and on in Cincinnati and today you can see his murals commissioned by Nicholas Longworth at the Taft Museum, the former home of the Longworths.

Of course Harriet Beecher Stowe went on to write *Uncle Tom's Cabin* and let all the world know the horrors of slavery. Some say her book was partially responsible for the end of slavery.

Circuses, steamboats, pig races, cotton mills, the Dumas House, the Willberforce Settlement, the Cincinnati Female Academy, The Western Female Institute and of course, the Underground Railroad all actually existed. The newspapers, *The Philanthropist* and the *Cincinnati Daily Post*, were active at this time. And, there really was a mob that attacked the printing shop of *The Philanthropist*. The Runaway Slave advertisement is from an actual document and Littsie's prayer is truly an old Irish prayer.

Yes, there was Christmas and I like to think that somehow Dan was real.